Daisy Morrow, Super-sleuth!

The Second One:

The Strange Case of the
Exploding Dolly-trolley

R T GREEN

R TGRGEN

Other books...

The Daisy Morrow Series:

The first one – The Root of All Evil
The second one – The Strange Case of the Exploding Dolly-trolley
The third one – A Very Unexpected African Adventure
The fourth one - Pirates of Great Yarmouth: Curse of the Crimson Heart
The sixth one – Call of Duty: The Wiltingham Enigma
The Box Set – books 1-3

Pale Moon: Season 1:

Episode 1: Rising
Episode 2: Falling
Episode 3: Broken
Episode 4: Phoenix
Episode 5: Jealousy
Episode 6: Homecoming
Episode 7: Fearless
Episode 8: Infinity

Season 2:

Episode 9: Phantom
Episode 10: Endgame
Episode 11: Desperation
Episode 12: Feral
Episode 13: Unbreakable
Episode 14: Phenomenal
Episode 15: Newborn
Episode 16: Evermore

The Starstruck Series -

Starstruck: Somewhere to call Home
Starstruck: The Prequel

(Time to say Goodbye)
Starstruck: The Disappearance of Becca
Starstruck: The Rock
Starstruck: Ghosts, Ghouls and Evil Spirits
Starstruck: The Combo – books 1-3

The Raven Series –

Raven: No Angel!
Raven: Unstoppable
Raven: Black Rose
Raven: The Combo – books 1-3

Little Cloud
Timeless
Ballistic
Cry of an Angel
The Hand of Time
Wisp
The Standalones

Contents

COME AND JOIN US!

We'd love you to become a VIP Reader.

Our intro library is the most generous in publishing!
Join our mail list and grab it all for free.
We really do appreciate every single one of you,
so there's always a freebie or two coming along,
news and updates, advance reads of new releases...

Head here to get started...
rtgreen.net

10

Introduction

This is the second book in the Daisy Morrow series. As you might have seen from the first one, Daisy is nothing like you might expect; she's funny, feisty, and has a tendency to get herself in sticky situations. And she definitely has a wicked side!

Before she retired, Daisy had a job very few people ever have, and although in the last year she's done her best to leave her legacy behind, somehow it manages to keep lurking in the shadows... in more ways than one!

Those of you who know my work will be aware that with the RTG brand, the unexpected is always around the next corner. Daisy is no exception, and is very probably even more so.

I hope she will make you smile, and maybe even gasp in surprise and shake your head a little. If she does, that will make me happy!

Please let us know what you think, either by email, or ideally by writing a review. Every comment is gratefully received... and is listened to!

Enjoy,
Richard

Daisy Morrow: Super-sleuth!

The Strange Case of the Exploding Dolly-trolley

Chapter 1

Two weeks have passed since Finn and his henchmen were caught red-handed. Two weeks where life seemed to drag itself slowly back to normal. At least, as normal as it ever got where Daisy was concerned.

It had taken her and Aidan the first of those weeks to come to terms with the fact the sting had actually worked, and then to slide gently down the other side of their somewhat dangerous high. As Daisy had said, the day after they got back from Morston Quay... 'Thirty years ago I would have breezed through all that without batting an eyelid. I think I might be getting too old for this, dear.'

Aidan had very gently told her he agreed, but knew better than to use those actual words. He just reminded her she *officially* retired eleven years ago, and the whole point of moving to the west-Norfolk village of Great Wiltingham was so they could enjoy *wilting* in peace.

It hadn't sat easily with Daisy, and Mother Nature seemed to confirm the Gods of Destiny were not in accord on that one, six days of grey cloud and almost-incessant rain making some kind of point. But she finally had to admit they were both right, despite the fact she (and Aidan) would have to put up with itchy feet and even itchier fingers for some months to come.

But reality has a nasty habit of not taking any notice of even the most reluctant of decisions... as Daisy and Aidan were about to find out, in the most brutal of ways.

The days of rain were followed by a week of sunshine and warm September temperatures, and Daisy had just started believing the gods of her destiny were at long last settling down, and finally allowing her to have a normal retirement.

Aidan was still sleeping at the cottage. Because of Daisy's previous job and the very unfortunate incident in London three years previously, when they'd moved to the village they bought separate houses. They spent their days together, but mostly when night fell they slept in their own homes.

Despite the fact they'd been married for thirty-five years.

It was Daisy's insistence, with Aidan's reluctant agreement. The serious incident three years ago, when they still lived in London, was connected to her previous employment. In her career at MI6 she'd inevitably made a few enemies. She could easily list a handful of people who might one day seek revenge, at some point when she was perhaps least expecting it.

It came with devastating effect. Daisy and Aidan weren't harmed, but someone very close to them suffered. Their daughter Celia bore the brunt of the retribution, but in a way neither of them expected. And in the kind of way that still didn't have closure.

But the incident was a tragic reminder that Daisy's past could also be her present. Now, at the age of seventy-one, she still found herself wary of every shadow that might turn out to not be a shadow at all.

For two years after the incident she and Aidan fought reluctantly with the options, but eventually it was clear only one alternative stood a chance of working long term. So a year ago they'd moved together but separately to Great Wiltingham, purchasing two houses just a few hundred yards from each other, and putting their wedding rings into a velvet box that never left Daisy's bedside table drawer.

Daisy reverted to her maiden name, and as far as anyone in Norfolk knew, she and Aidan were simply the best of friends. Her previous employers made sure their official records were purged, and their new life of peaceful retirement became a reality.

Aidan had initially protested that Daisy would spend most nights alone, wanting to be there to protect her if the worst happened. But as she pointed out, she was far more equipped to protect herself than he was. In the end he grudgingly accepted that, given the situation, she was probably right.

Aidan had spent his adult life working as an accountant. Daisy hadn't.

For the first year in Great Wiltingham, all was as peaceful as it was intended to be. Daisy played the role of the doddery old biddie to perfection, driving around the village on a mobility scooter, even though she really didn't need to. Then one day, everything changed.

She and Aidan discovered the village was being abused by criminals using it as a delivery-point for hard drugs. Something which, in their case, was way too close to home for comfort.

The identity of the mysterious bulk supplier became an obsession for Daisy. Which culminated two weeks ago with him being caught red-handed, with a little help from a young policewoman called Sarah Lowry, who found Daisy's approach to crime-solving way more exciting than mundane police work!

Those two weeks of relative peace later, life had returned to something approaching normal. But their scary adventure had brought changes. Although the bad guys were nothing to do with the enemies Daisy had made in the past, they brought her a strange, unexpected kind of nervousness. Aidan had moved in while the sting was under way, and fourteen days after it was over, he still hadn't moved out.

Daisy was getting used to shuggling up with him at night. So much so that three days ago, she'd ever-so-vaguely suggested they might have been wrong to buy separate houses. But as usual, it came out in Daisy-speak. Which didn't fool Aidan for a second...

'Dear, I've been thinking,' she said quietly, sitting on her stool at the island unit in the kitchen, eating her comfort food of cheese on toast with added pepperoni and jalapenos.

'Should I be worried?' he grinned.

'Maybe. You seem to be enjoying sleeping here.'

'I thought you'd never ask.'

'I haven't asked anything yet.'

'Haven't you?' He put an arm around her shoulders and gave her a gentle kiss, which was only slightly jalapeno-flavoured.

'No fooling you, is there?'

'I do have a brain the size of a small galaxy, according to you.'

16

She took a sip of her coffee, trying not to grin. 'Maybe sleeping in separate houses *has* outlived its usefulness.'

'It was never *useful*, just necessary. And annoying.'

'Ok, galactic-brain. So you've sussed me. What are you going to do about it?'

'You leaving the decision to me?'

'Yes dear.'

So that morning, Aidan had left at nine to meet the estate agent at the bungalow, and be there while they planted the 'For Sale' board. At nine-thirty, Daisy had wandered across the gravel drive and opened the white five-barred gate. Robert James, the service agent in Kings Lynn, was coming at ten to take her mobility scooter away for service, and with the gate open he could drive his van straight in.

She was just about to head back inside when she heard a cheerful *'Cooeee'*, and turned back to the road to see Maisie walking past, waving manically. 'Lovely morning, Daisy.'

She wandered over to the little gate next to the big gate. 'Out for a constitutional, Maisie?' she said, and then saw her friend wasn't alone.

Maisie was widely regarded as the dottiest resident in the village. Some even saw her as the village crazie, but in reality she wasn't crazy at all. Rather eccentric maybe, and bordering on acute dottiness... a fact borne out by the fact she was passing by taking her cat for a walk.

Daisy tried not to giggle at the strange sight of the furball on a red lead. 'Yes, Maisie, it is a lovely morning. Taking Brutus for a walk I see.'

'Oh yes. He's not been out for a few days, you know.'

'But you put him out every night.'

'I know, but it's not the same. He likes his walks on the leash.'

'So I see,' Daisy said, quite astonished to see Brutus standing dutifully quietly by his owner's side. 'I have to say, he is good on the lead...'

Maisie looked quite indignant. 'Of course he is. I did train him well you know. Even though when I got up this morning, he was a bit spooked. He even hissed at me. But he soon calmed down after I gave him a bit of fillet steak and promised to take him for a walk. Anyway, I'm now going. He'll be needing a pee soon, and I haven't refilled his cat tray yet.'

Daisy tried to keep the amused shake of her head from Maisie's line of vision, but her dotty friend was already walking away so it wasn't that difficult. 'I guess you trained him not to pee up lampposts then?' she called after the slightly-portly woman in the polyester skirt and flower-patterned blouse.

She looked back and tut-tutted. 'Daisy, sometimes I wonder about you. He's a cat!'

Chapter 2

Daisy headed back into the kitchen, and picked up the keys to the dolly-trolley, the mobility scooter affectionately christened by Aidan when he modified it to go faster than any dolly-trolley ever had. She'd decided to move it out of its little open-fronted enclosure sitting next to the garage, so it would be sitting waiting for Robert to drive it straight into his van when he arrived.

She didn't quite make it. As she walked across the drive towards the enclosure, a car turned into the open gateway, and the cheerful toot of the horn was accompanied by an even more cheerful smile. Daisy turned on her heels just before she reached the enclosure, and walked over to the car.

The young woman dressed in her pristine police uniform dropped the window, and smiled a warm smile. Her big blue eyes seemed to sparkle in the morning sunlight, and the flawless skin on her pretty face appeared to glow with vitality.

She looked a million miles from the limp rag doll who had struggled out of the engine room hatch of Finn's boat two weeks ago. In all fairness, she had just been through thirty-six hours of stowaway hell. Daisy knew all too well it took a week or two to recover from ordeals like that.

'I wasn't expecting to see you today, Sarah,' she smiled.

'Not stopping. On my way to the station, later shift today. Just wanted to tell you Burrows read your eight-page interview report we *almost-truthfully* wrote. Then he sighed like he didn't really believe most of it, and told me it would be filed away and ignored.'

'That was good of your boss,' said Daisy, only slightly-sarcastically.

'Quite honestly he's got so much on right now, organising the case with the CPS so that murderers and drug runners get their due sentences, he's not got time to bother about a couple of nosy old cronies like you two.'

It was said with a smile, and taken the same way. 'I bet the grumpy DCI wishes he had got the time though... I can just imagine the delight on his face when he reads us the riot act and tells us to leave police business to the police in future.'

'Yeah well, Daisy. Maybe if he'd had the time it might have been the best thing?'

Daisy let out a huge, genuine sigh. 'I know. I'm too old for those kind of shenanigans, as everyone keeps telling me... including my own gut.'

'Somehow I wonder if you'll truly listen to it, or to everyone else.'

'It's hard, Sarah... so hard. You got time for a coffee?'

'Wish I had. Gotta get to the station. Thanks anyway. We still on for dinner tomorrow?'

'You bet. Aidan is rooting through his cookbooks to find something special.'

'He's a good man. Taking care of you as he does, and then having to go home every night?'

It was a question, a leading one. Designed to provoke a certain reply. It came.

'Actually, he's not going home anymore. He's round at the bungalow now, supervising the planting of the sale board. He decided two houses were a bit silly.'

'*He* decided?'

'Well...'

Sarah grinned. 'I'm delighted for you both. It's the right thing. I'm glad you asked him to stay permanently.'

'Um... I...' Daisy started to protest at the inference, but then realised there were no words to argue with. Sarah had got it spot on.

The window whirred up, and with a cheery and slightly self-satisfied wave, she backed out of the drive and drove away. Five seconds later, Robert's van was backing in. He pulled up next to Daisy, and opened the driver's door.

'Mornin', Flower,' he grinned cheerily. He was the only person other than Aidan to call her that. In his early sixties and a true Norfolk boy, he was close to retirement, but rather like Daisy wasn't exactly looking forward to it. Mobility scooters were his life, and the vast majority of his customers were those who, unlike Daisy, actually needed his help.

'Morning, Bob. You want a coffee before you go?' she smiled to him.

'I shouldn't, got a lot on today. But if you be twisting my arm...'

'I'll put the kettle on.' She glanced down to the keys in her hand. 'I was just about to pull it out for you, but Sarah came, and then you were here.'

'No worries. I'll drive it into the van while you make that coffee.'

He opened the rear doors and pressed the button to drop the tail-lift. Daisy handed him the keys and headed into the kitchen, filled the kettle. Aidan would be back any time, so she made sure she boiled enough water for him too.

Through the open side window she heard the crunch of boots on gravel, and knew Robert was heading to the enclosure to fetch the dolly-trolley. For a second she

21

thought about hurrying out to remind him Aidan had modified the motor somewhat, on her insistence that it didn't go fast enough. But then she realised it was too late anyway, as the whirr of the motor told her he was already driving it out of the enclosure.

Three seconds later, another noise filled her ears. Something that drowned out everything else.

A loud explosion reverberated around the driveway, and shook the house to its very foundations.

Chapter 3

For a second, Daisy froze. For a second, her brain tried to tell her it was a huge, sudden clap of thunder. But as she found some movement and ran towards the side door, she knew all too well it wasn't Mother Nature making another point.

Then she cried out as her frantic eyes fell on the drive, and her footsteps suddenly welded themselves to the outside step. A head that tried not to accept what her eyes were telling her began to spin. She clutched the doorframe to stop herself keeling over.

It was like a scene from Afghanistan. The drive and the whole area between the house and the garage were littered with smouldering wreckage.

The wreckage of her mobility scooter.

It felt like she whispered something, but she couldn't be sure. Her head was reeling with images that couldn't possibly be, couldn't possibly have happened in a peaceful Norfolk village. She closed her eyes a moment, tried to pull her senses into line.

When she opened them again, there was nothing different to see.

She stepped onto the drive, like it was going to swallow her up. *Where was Bob?* She staggered a few steps further, her eyes flicking furtively around like she was back in a war zone. Then she saw him.

Slumped against the corner of the house, fifteen feet away from his van, he wasn't moving. Daisy ran to him, lifted a lifeless hand to check his pulse, and cried out again.

There was no pulse. His head was slumped across his chest, so she couldn't see his eyes.

She reached out a hand to lift his head, but then took it away again. She didn't want to see his eyes, knew there was no way to revive him. The seat of the dolly-trolley lay on the ground five feet away from him. It was virtually intact, deliberately over-built to help protect the mobility scooter's users from any accidents that might befall them.

Judging by the wreckage all around her, the scooter had exploded, violently. The seat had acted like an ejector seat, but had propelled its occupant upwards so viciously, no human being could have ever withstood the sudden force.

Bob had been dead before he even hit the ground.

'Daisy!'

A frantic cry filled the silent air. Aidan was running through the open gate, his face creased with concern and disbelief. Daisy struggled to her feet as he reached her, and fell into his arms like a rag doll.

'Oh my god... are you ok?'

The words to answer him didn't seem to want to come. She just nodded against his shoulder as he held her tight, and then the tears came. She felt his hand close around the back of her head, pull her even closer to him as he allowed her to cry it out.

'I was just walking back when I heard the explosion... Bob... is he...'

Again she could find no words, just nodded through the sobs. He eased her away, pulled the phone from his pocket. 'We have to call the emergency services, dear...'

He answered the voice on the other end. 'Yes, I need to report an explosion... there's been an accident... in Great Wiltingham...'

'Is that Fern Cottage, sir?

'Yes... how did you know?'

'It's just been called in sir, by a neighbour. Police are already on their way.'

'Ok, thank you.' He killed the call, focused sad eyes on Daisy. Their heads had been close enough together for her to hear the conversation. She finally found a whisper.

'Tell me this is just an awful nightmare, Dip.'

He shook his head despondently. 'I wish I could.'

A few nosy neighbours were gathering at the gateway, calling out to them, a small sea of shaking heads trying to get themselves around what had happened. But then a car appeared behind them, and the sea of bodies parted to allow it through.

Sarah brought her car to a stop behind Bob's van, wrenched open the driver's door and ran to Daisy and Aidan. 'Burrows called me when I was halfway to work, told me they'd had a call and to get over to you. He'll be here in a few minutes... oh my god, Daisy... thank goodness you're alright. *Oh...*'

She caught sight of the body. And from the look on her friend's faces she realised not everyone had escaped unharmed. Daisy lifted her eyes to the sky, ran a hand across her mouth, and confirmed Sarah's worst thoughts. 'Someone took the fall for me, I think.'

Still the ever-growing crowd at the gate was demanding to know what was happening. Aidan looked like he wasn't quite sure which reality he was in, but knew the onlookers weren't helping. 'Sarah...'

She swallowed hard. 'Yes, I know.' She switched into Officer Lowry mode and walked over to the gate, trying her hardest to exude the confidence that had been shocked out

25

of her. 'Ok, everyone. Move away please... this is a crime scene now. *Move!'*

The final word was virtually screamed out, her emotions once again at an all-time high. It had the desired effect, the onlookers moved back and thirty seconds later a cacophony of sirens wailed into Walcotts Lane. Two police cars tried to make their way onto the drive, but the devastation didn't allow them to get very far. An ambulance from the Queen Elizabeth Hospital in Kings Lynn pulled up in the lane, right in front of the drive.

Two paramedics carrying trauma kit headed to the body, but it was only seconds before they both shook their heads, and covered it with a thick blanket while they went to fetch the stretcher.

Burrows stepped out of the first car, glancing around in disbelief, and ambled over to the two elderly residents still clasped in each other's arms.

'Well, Daisy, we meet again. And so soon.'

Chapter 4

'Morning, DCI Burrows. I won't say *good*.'

'No, it certainly isn't that.' He cast his sunken eyes around the drive. 'Had a bit of an accident, have we?'

Daisy wiped away the tears. *'This was no accident,'* she growled. 'And I'd thank you not to be so flippant, Inspector. A man is dead, in case you haven't noticed.'

He nodded his head, like he agreed with her. 'I'm sorry... shall we go inside, and you can tell me what happened?'

They made their way into the house. The four officers who'd arrived with Burrows had closed the gate, and were already sticking streamers of black and yellow tape everywhere. A van had pulled into the drive, and three other people were donning protective suits, getting ready to sift through what was left of the dolly-trolley.

Some of the leftovers were still smoking.

Aidan poured three brandies. Burrows downed his in one go, even though he was on duty. Daisy slumped onto her stool at the island unit, took tiny sips of hers with both hands around the glass, looking and feeling like a little girl who'd just done something really bad.

She told Burrows what little she knew. Until the explosion, nothing had seemed out of the ordinary. After the explosion, nothing was ordinary at all. Her mind was already racing, trying to work out who was the most likely to want her dead.

The inspector didn't know the truth about her past, and she was reluctant to tell him any more than she absolutely had to. But jaded and battle-weary as he was, he was no fool.

27

'So who would want you dead, Daisy?

She glanced to Aidan over the top of her brandy glass, asking him an unspoken question, unsure how much she should say. He nodded, and came to her rescue. 'Daisy used to work for MI6, Inspector. Back in the day she was a field agent, and inevitably made a few enemies. She's been retired from active duty some time now. More than that is above your pay grade, I'm afraid. Classified and all that, you know.'

Burrows nodded like he was being fobbed off. 'I see. So *if* someone sabotaged your mobility scooter, how am I supposed to discover who it was?'

'Quite frankly, you have a difficult task, Inspector. But we cannot help you any further.'

'Hmm... I could investigate *you* instead, Mr. Henderson.'

Aidan shook his head disdainfully. 'Feel free, Mr. Burrows. But do you really think I would murder my own wife?'

Daisy groaned, and he realised what he'd said as soon as the words came out of his gob. DCI Burrows narrowed his eyes at him. He hadn't got to the heights of a DCI by missing stuff.

'Wife? I thought you two were... just good friends?'

Aidan knew his verbal slip meant he had to say something. 'We've been married for thirty-five years, Inspector. After an unfortunate incident three years ago, MI6 expunged our records. And that is *really* all you're getting.'

'So, the plot thickens...' Burrows was about to say something else, but one of the officers in protective clothing walked into the kitchen. 'Sir, there's something unusual you should see.'

He was carrying a few mangled bits of motor in his hands. Aidan and Daisy glanced furtively at each other, and let out collective groans. Burrows however was no expert when it came to mobility scooters. 'What am I looking at, Phillips?'

'Well, sir… I'm not sure if it's significant, but this motor is not standard issue for this type of vehicle. It's a lot bigger than the manufacturers fit.'

'Really?'

Aidan threw his hands up in the air. 'Ok… fair cop. I fitted a bigger motor. Like they do for racing lawnmowers. But there's no way it would have exploded like that.'

'*Racing lawnmowers?* You're kidding me.'

'Believe it, Inspector. Google it.'

Burrows shook his head, but there were more important things on his mind. 'So are you saying that particular scooter was modified to travel faster than the lawful speed, Mr. Henderson?'

'Um…'

Daisy couldn't let Aidan handle the embarrassment alone. 'I asked him to, Inspector. Well, I didn't give him any peace, if I'm honest. It was just a little tweak…'

'A little tweak which made it illegal.'

'Well…'

Sarah appeared in the door. 'Sir, we've secured the scene. And we found this, on the lawn.'

Daisy breathed a sigh of relief. In a tragic situation, it was at least a saved-by-the-bell moment when it came to the minor fact of being prosecuted for driving an illegal vehicle. She'd seen the object Sarah was holding before. Not that particular one, but ones very similar, back in another life.

'It's a detonator,' she whispered.

'Yes, it is. Sir, it's beginning to look like the scooter was rigged with a C-4 explosive, arranged to go off when the throttle was opened wide. It's easy enough to do if the detonator is connected to the throttle mechanism. Would you like to see what we've found outside, sir?'

'I guess. Show me what you've got, Lowry.'

Sarah glanced back and winked as the two of them stepped back outside. Daisy mouthed a silent *thank you* as they disappeared, and then held her glass out to Aidan.

'I think I need a refill, if you'd be so kind, dear.'

Chapter 5

Burrows and the four officers who arrived with him headed back to the station. There was little to do at the scene of the crime other than give the victims a ticket for driving an illegal vehicle, and that even he wasn't prepared to do, given the circumstances.

The forensics team was still there, searching painstakingly for clues the force of the explosion wasn't going to allow them to find. Whoever set the bomb knew exactly what they were doing; a big enough explosion tended to destroy most of the evidence. Sarah was still at the scene too, left on crowd-control duties, and victim liaison.

Burrows was all too aware she was the best officer for the job, given who the victims were.

It was late afternoon, and the sun had disappeared behind the trees, throwing long shadows across the drive. Daisy had spent a couple of hours in her bedroom, officially taking a nap. Sarah and Aidan both knew she would do nothing of the sort.

There were far more important things she had to try and force her head around.

She wandered back into the open-plan living area to find the two of them sitting at the island unit, sipping mugs of coffee. Both stood up as they saw her, but Daisy only had one destination in mind right then. She pulled Sarah into her, held her tight and whispered in her ear.

'I need to thank you for saving my life.'

'But... I didn't do anything except call in to say hello.'

'Exactly.' Daisy smiled a thank you to Aidan as he handed her a cup of freshly-brewed black coffee. 'That's what saved my life.'

'I don't understand.'

'I was just heading to the enclosure to pull the scooter out ready for Bob when you turned up. I saw you, so I didn't get as far as the scooter. Then he arrived just before you left, and said he'd drive it into the van while I made his coffee.' She let out a little shudder, reached for Aidan's hand.

'*Oh my god*... so me turning up stopped you moving the scooter...' He eyes misted up. 'But by default, that means that because of me Bob lost his life...'

'You can't blame yourself, Sarah. Someone was clearly destined to get it... there but for the grace of god and all that.'

Sarah turned away, put both hands on the worktop like she needed support. 'It doesn't make it easier to live with though.'

Aidan slipped a hand around her shoulders. 'No, it doesn't. But in truth, living with the death of anyone is never easy.'

Daisy headed to the alcohol cupboard, lifted out the brandy and three glasses. 'Don't use the *on-duty* card, Sarah. We all need another one.'

Aidan had already noticed the look in her eyes. It was one he recognised. One that he knew her time alone in the bedroom had put there. 'I suppose you're about to tell us you've been thinking, dear?'

'Well I was never going to sleep, was I?'

'Course you weren't, Flower.'

'You know me too well, dear.'

'I do, and I can see the shock of the day's events has been replaced by another emotion.'

Sarah sipped her brandy, throwing a questioning glance to both her friends at the same time. 'I've still not tuned into your telepathic link yet, so is someone going to tell me what you're talking about?'

'Daisy has got that look again,' said Aidan, slightly nervously.

'Do I need to ask *what look*?' said Sarah, in a resigned and slightly-frustrated kind of way.

Daisy sat at her stool, *the look* turning to a narrow-eyed stare. 'Let's face it, the police... no offence, Sarah... aren't going to find anything to give them a clue who did it. And we, nor anyone at MI6 who remembers what happened three years ago, aren't going to reveal any sensitive information. So there aren't many avenues left for bringing the perpetrator to justice.'

'Except..?'

'Except the one which I'm not prepared to let the police handle anyway.'

Aidan lowered his head. 'I had a horrible feeling...'

'What?' cried Sarah, still floundering in the almost-dark.

'There's no choice now, and quite frankly I'm not sure I'd want one even if there was. I'm going to have to investigate my own murder!'

33

Chapter 6

It was time to sleep, but neither Daisy nor Aidan felt too confident about it actually happening. Sitting up in bed sipping hot chocolate and looking like the elderly married couple they really were, snuggling down to dream of fluffy white rabbits lolloping around a grassy meadow was the last thing on their minds.

All was quiet. Aidan had rigged the security lights to stay on constantly, and earlier they'd noticed a police car parked in Walcotts Lane just opposite the drive. Then it had gone, but was back again when they looked out just before falling into bed.

They both knew even the best intentions of Burrows, or maybe the insistence of Sarah, couldn't actually protect them from the kind of people who most likely had it in for Daisy, but somehow the police presence was still comforting.

It felt like someone cared.

Aidan had suggested they spend the night in his bungalow, but Daisy had declined. She pointed out that whoever had discovered where she lived would almost certainly know where Aidan lived too, and his small bungalow sitting right next to the tiny alley was an easier target than the cottage. Right then the thatched house looked like it had its own pool of artificial daylight, and a police presence to deter intruders.

There was another reason. The last thing Daisy was going to allow was that whoever had wanted her dead would get the consolation prize of at least knowing he'd driven her out of her own home.

He'd failed to murder her by a whisker. He wasn't going to intimidate her, come what may.

Aidan broke the silence, up to then punctuated only by sips of hot chocolate. 'So have we got a shortlist yet, dear?'

She nodded. 'Oh yes. Three. But one stands high above the rest.'

'I think I know who you're going to say.'

'Course you do. Roland Spence.'

He nodded. 'That doesn't come as any surprise, given that he made a very public promise to get his revenge when he was arrested. But that was three years ago, dear... and he's been in prison ever since.'

She rested her mug on the duvet, sighed out the words. 'I know, and some may say he got his revenge with Celia. But I'm not so sure that was enough for him. From what I hear he's virtually running Belmarsh now, and he never got his hands dirty with things like directly murdering someone anyway. That's why he was so hard to catch, because he was too clever to ever be *directly* involved in anything.'

'I suppose it would just take a phone call, with a guard on his payroll paid to look the other way.'

'Exactly. Getting put away doesn't stand a hope in hell of actually stopping him doing anything illegal. I should have shot him when I had...'

'You never actually met him, dear. Not in person. You seriously damaged his empire years before the... Celia thing. It was the guy we did catch who squealed and actually implicated him. Sadly, too late to protect Celia. But you never got to shoot Roland Spence because you never came face-to-face with him... and it wouldn't have looked so good on your CV anyway.'

'Stuff the CV. I still wish I had...'

35

'Why are you so sure it's him?'

She let out a little shudder, reached for Aidan's hand. 'You weren't in the courtroom when he was sentenced. The pointed finger, the look he gave me...'

He pulled her close to him. 'Ok, try not to think about it. So how do we go about investigating this? If he did organise the hit, there doesn't seem to be any clues to who did it, or who ordered it.'

'I know. It's a bugger, as you would say.'

'Ok. Forensics have gone, we've got our home to ourselves. I'm not sure there's anything to find, but tomorrow, if you're up to it, we'll comb the drive and the garden, just in case. Deal?'

'Deal.'

The morning dawned bright and sunny. The mood in the cottage was anything but. After a night spent fighting fraught dreams, and a breakfast Daisy, uncharacteristically, could only nibble at, they braved the outside world.

For Daisy it was nothing short of hell, at first. Forensics had taken away all traces of the dolly-trolley and Bob's van, but there was plenty of evidence to point to where the tragedy had taken place. The scooter had been only feet away from the enclosure and the garage it was sitting up against; the blast had ripped the frail roof away from the open-fronted shelter, and singed the once-white paint of the garage doors.

For her it was a harsh reminder that someone she knew had lost the life she was meant to lose.

Aidan was a rock, holding her close and asking multiple times if she wanted to carry on. As always, his closeness helped her come to terms with what had happened. And as

36

they went into their second hour of combing the garden for clues, someone else helped too.

Roland Spence.

Daisy didn't hate many people; the number of human beings on that list was less than the fingers on one hand. But she hated Roland Spence. Way back when she'd been instrumental in bringing his empire down, his suave demeanour that bordered on creepy was something that gave her nightmares.

He believed he was rich and powerful enough to be untouchable. The son of parents who had become rich in legal ways, he went off the rails at university, the end result of too much money turning to too much power that he was too young to handle.

But the damage was done, and he'd already realised he could become even more rich and powerful in the kind of ways his parents hadn't. Years later when he'd built his questionable empire, it was a massive shock to him that he'd been ultimately brought down by someone he thought he could trust.

Daisy had been the agent who turned a hardened criminal into an informer. She'd never met Spence, not in person, until the trial. But for the eighteen months that led up to her touching the untouchable, she'd spent every waking hour getting to know every tiny detail of the man and his empire.

It wasn't a pleasant learning experience.

Yes, he'd sworn to get his revenge. And three years ago he took it. Tragically, he decided to go for those Daisy loved rather than Daisy herself. He'd had time in prison to research the person he knew was responsible for his downfall, discover her few weak points. He'd had time to plan his retribution to the last detail.

Unfortunately, the last detail didn't include the unpredictability of the person he employed to carry out a swift, seamless job. The callous thug saw an opportunity, and took it. And what should have been a quick, bitter end turned into something that still didn't have an end at all.

Right there, right then, that wasn't the issue for Daisy. Roland Spence was the nasty piece of work who had instigated the revenge three years ago, and had now somehow discovered Daisy's new life, and decided it was too peaceful and comfortable for him to ignore.

So as she stood up and headed back to the house to make coffees, Daisy did so with a grim but determined smile on her face. He'd instigated tragedy again, but got the wrong person. It was the kick in the butt she needed. The push to take her past the obvious emotions, and into the positive ones.

He would get his just desserts once again, from the waitress he never expected to serve them. That, suddenly, was the only thing that mattered.

'I think we've drawn a blank, dear,' said an aching Aidan.

'We weren't really expecting to find anything the police had missed.'

'It's still disappointing though, Flower.'

Daisy let out another shudder. She and Aidan were standing on the drive, sipping their coffees in the September sunshine. She'd just allowed her eyes to focus on the garage doors, and the awful memory they invoked.

'Dear, do we have any white paint? I don't think I want to look at brown scorch marks anymore.'

He squeezed her hand and smiled. 'On it right now.'

He headed to the garage, and then Daisy noticed movement at the front gate. She narrowed slightly-misty eyes to try and see who it was, although it was obvious enough.

Someone was standing on the pavement, waving frantically but silently.

Chapter 7

'Maisie? No cooees today?'

As Daisy walked up to the pedestrian gate, the woman in the flowery blouse and the cream leggings a couple of sizes too big for her, frowned her confusion. 'You said if I shouted like a banshee the men in white coats would come for me.'

'I didn't mean… oh, never mind. You want a coffee? Kettle's just boiled.'

'Well I would dear, but there's black and yellow tape everywhere. I don't want to trample over a crime scene. I watch NCIS, you know.'

Daisy ripped away the tape so the little gate was free. 'Quite honestly Maisie, I'm trying to pretend it isn't. Not exactly easy though. Come on in anyway.'

She trotted through the gate, picking up Brutus in her arms, looking somewhat spooked. The cat, not Maisie. 'Well I don't know Daisy, all this has really freaked Brutus out. The minute I tried to pull him through the gate, he *really* didn't like it.'

'Nothing to do with the fact he's a cat on a lead then, dear?' Daisy asked, only slightly sarcastically.

'Of course not,' Maisie said huffily as they wandered into the kitchen. 'I told you, he's good on the lead. And he never pees up lampposts either, before you ask again.'

'So why is he so spooked? He wanders round here most nights, quite happily.'

As if on cue, Brutus, still in Maisie's arms, let out a low, throaty growl.

'Wow, he's really not happy. Put him down, I'll sort him some milk.'

Maisie did as she was asked. 'He only likes semi-skimmed. Don't give him full cream or he'll get even more annoyed.'

'Yes Maisie, whatever you say.'

Brutus slunk over to the milk, looking every bit like the cat that hadn't got the cream. Maisie however had other things on her mind. 'I'm sorry to say this dear, but it has to be asked. Did Aidan really cause your mobility scooter to explode?'

'Maisie!'

'Well I'm sorry Daisy, but someone had to ask. It's what the whole village is saying.'

'What the fire-breathing dragon is saying, you mean?'

'Well... Matilda might be the root cause... if you pardon the pun.'

'Yes Maisie, it will take the village forever to get over the fact the police dug up her floribundas. But no, it wasn't a bigger motor, so you can get that out of your dotty head right now. It was a stick of C-4 explosive.'

Maisie looked at her wide-eyed. 'I don't understand. Why would Aidan want to blow up your scooter?'

'*He didn't...* oh for Christ's sake Maisie, get your head around this... it was *nothing* to do with Aidan, ok? Someone wanted to take revenge on me.'

'Was it Matilda?'

'*Maisie*... please stop this typically you train of thought. It wasn't Aidan, or anyone else in the village. Someone from my past... when I lived somewhere else... is responsible, ok? Is that sinking in?'

'There's no need to be so insulting. It's not my fault you upset someone enough to want to kill you.'

Daisy threw her arms in the air, and then sat on the stool next to Maisie and took her hand. 'I'm sorry. I'm not quite

41

myself right now. It's been almost too much to take. I didn't mean to shout at you, but just please accept that the person responsible doesn't even live in Norfolk, let alone this village.'

Maisie squeezed her hand, smiled. 'It's ok. I didn't come round yesterday because I knew you'd be upset, and you wouldn't want the village crazie butting in.'

'Oh Maisie... you're not the village crazie... even if you do take your cat for a walk sometimes. In some ways you're the sanest person I know... and a good friend too.'

'Thank you, dear. But talking of village crazies... you seem pretty sure you know who did it?'

Daisy ignored the inference. 'Yes, I have a pretty good idea. But for now, the less you know the better, Maisie. Having said that, please spread the news Aidan had nothing to do with it. Just keep it at that, *please?* Don't go telling everyone it was some sort of terrorist plot, ok?'

'I'm not an idiot, dear.'

Chapter 8

It was time for bed. Aidan had cooked his usual delicious dinner, and this time they'd both devoured it, and enjoyed it. Aidan looked happier, because his wife looked more like herself, and the steely determination to solve the mystery was back in her eyes.

Sarah had called, told them she was all but locked down at the station, attempting to keep her boss on the right track and discover the identity of the murderer, even though forensics had virtually come up with nothing to help them. She promised to call in the next day, before work.

Daisy had groaned to Aidan. Sarah and the police had nothing to go on. That wasn't exactly surprising, but it left Daisy with a very limited choice of options.

'I'm going to see Roland.'

'Dear, that's not the best idea. I doubt they'll grant you a visiting order anyway, given who he is.'

'They will if I say I'm his brief.'

'You can't be serious?'

'Have you got a better idea?'

'Well, no. But we don't even know if it's him for sure.'

'Why do you think I want to go see him?'

He sighed, already knowing nothing he could say would change her mind. 'Just promise me one thing. Sleep on that tonight, and then if you still feel the same in the cold light of day, I'll go with it. Deal?'

'Deal, dear,' she said. She almost followed it up with, '*but it won't make any difference*,' but decided against it.

She didn't sleep on it. Not anything she could call sleep, anyway. Aidan had dropped off, into a deep sleep exhaustion had helped him to find, but Daisy kept herself awake. It wasn't intentional, but having been virtually forced into the option of confronting Roland Spence through a lack of anything more concrete, all she could think about was how to persuade a sickly-smooth criminal to tell her what she needed to know.

She'd managed a fitful hour or so, but as she glanced at the clock and realised it was almost two in the morning, she realised drastic action might be called for. Aidan was fast asleep, but for over two hours she'd flicked from one side to the other, and discovered it was doing nothing but making sleep even harder to find.

She gave it up as a bad job, and padded quietly down the stairs to pour herself a get-to-sleep brandy. The light from the security lamps filtered through the windows and gave her enough to easily see by, but it wasn't enough to feel comfortable by. She flicked on every downstairs light she could find, and headed to the bottle, poured herself a large, purely medicinal one.

She didn't fancy taking it to bed and drinking it in the almost-dark, so she sat on her usual stool next to the island unit, wrapped both hands around the glass, and took a couple of sips.

And then she heard a noise at the outside door.

She froze, just for a second. For another second she considered running to the bedroom, grabbing the AK-47 from the corner of the room where she's placed it the previous night, just in case.

But then logic took over. The noise sounded like something was scratching at the bottom of the door, scrabbling to get in, not shoving it violently off its hinges.

She stood up, inched her way to the door, listened in the silence with her ear close to the bottom.

Whatever it was, it wasn't human. Or maybe a foot-high dwarf, but that wasn't exactly likely. Hesitantly she reached out a hand, felt for the key sitting on the dresser next to the door, picked it up and stretched her arm out to the lock.

Then she hesitated. What if it was the murderer again, pretending to be an innocent animal? She shook her head, trying to clear the feeling she was getting as dotty as Maisie. Someone capable of taking a life wasn't going to scratch meekly at a door to gain entry.

She slipped the key into the lock, turned it, and then grabbed the black cast-iron handle and eased it down. The door opened, just an inch. Nothing happened. She opened it another inch. Something happened.

A hairy paw wrapped around the tiny opening, doing everything it could to try and make it bigger.

'Brutus!'

Daisy opened the door wide enough to let the cat in, and then closed and locked it again. The cat looked like he'd just found his oasis in a scary desert, meowed his gratitude in the kind of way that was also a vague kind of grumble.

She poured him a bowl of milk, went to stroke his long hair as she put in on the floor for him. For a second he grumbled at her petting too, but then seemed to relent and allowed her to touch him.

'I don't know about me, you don't seem to be yourself either, Brutus,' she said softly as she left him to his milk and sat back with the brandy.

She watched him idly as he lapped up his semi-skimmed, and a frown started to furrow her brow. A British Longhair, rather like his owner he was getting on in years. Ever since she'd known them both, Brutus had hardly lived up to his name, never acting in a way that could be described as anything but docile. Except when Maisie decided to give him a bath, anyway.

Even when he was taken for a walk by his owner, he seemed to take everything in his stride, as it were. Yet ever since the night before last, according to Maisie, he'd been spooked.

The night before last.

She stood up slowly, knelt down quietly next to Brutus so as not to spook him any more, and shook her head slowly. 'Is there something you want to tell me, Brutus?' she whispered.

He didn't answer, just finished the milk, and then turned his old head as far back as he could, and tried to nuzzle at his collar. Something about it was bugging him, although it was hardly surprising. A red collar meant for a small dog, it was thick, and covered with chrome studs.

Daisy shook her head again. She'd commented just a few days ago that he looked more like a Rottweiler, much to his owner's disgust. She'd stopped short of quipping that he was a sheep in wolf's clothing, but right then the docile cat seemed to be disturbed by the collar.

But as she watched him struggling, it wasn't the collar he was bugged with. He was trying to get to the fur underneath it.

She reached out a hand, stroked him again. Her heart began to race as her brain started to put two and two together. Was she making five? Maybe. But she already knew he ambled round to the cottage most nights. Had he stumbled on the murderous intruder, the night before last?

Slowly she undid the collar, not an easy task given his long hair. Somehow he knew there was something under it

46

he didn't like. '*How I wish you could talk, Brutus,*' she whispered, being as gentle as she could.

The collar was free. She lifted it away. Brutus meowed, like he was grateful, started to nuzzle his nose into the part of his fur he hadn't been able to get to. Daisy stroked his head, easing it away from his neck. If by some freak chance there was something there, the last thing she needed was the cat swallowing it.

At first she could see nothing, and could feel her heart sinking again. Then, as she explored his fur with her fingers, she came across something. She frowned, unwilling to let her heart believe it was a significant find.

A few strands of his hair were matted together by something, just on the edge of where his collar would normally sit. She'd seen that something before, many times in her previous life.

Surely not?

She picked him up, cradled him in her arms so he couldn't lick it away. He didn't protest, probably just too grateful his dog-collar was gone. She walked to the utensil's drawer, lifted out a small pair of scissors.

'I'm so sorry, my friend. But I need this tiny bit of you.'

She stood him up on the island top, stroked him again. Then, before he knew what was happening, she snipped off the all-important strands of hair. He meowed again, but didn't growl. She stroked him again, thanked him for his help, and fastened the collar back in place, much to his disgust.

Then he looked a little more grateful as he was fed a slice of ham from the fridge, before the door was opened and he was persuaded to go and continue his night's foraging. Daisy slumped back on her stool, her mind racing with a possible scenario that *just possibly* could be the right scenario.

Had Brutus come across the murderer, just as he was tinkering with the dolly-trolley? Had he realised it wasn't the usual sight he would see at the cottage? Had he got too curious, been roughly shoved away, and retaliated with his claws?

It was almost too much to hope for. But as Daisy found a small sealy-bag and carefully placed the hair inside, she knew it was at least a fair possibility.

The strands of hair were matted together by a drop of dried blood.

Chapter 9

Daisy and Aidan heard the crunch of wheels on gravel, and a moment later Sarah walked through the open kitchen door and hugged them both.

'I'm so sorry I didn't get over yesterday. Burrows had me working overtime, not that it turns out we have much to go on.'

Daisy shoved a coffee in her hands, and then nodded to the tiny clear plastic bag on the worktop. 'We might have something worthy of your time. But we're going to ask if you can keep whatever you find between us, for now at least.'

'Daisy?' She picked up the little bag, peered at its contents. 'It's a few strands of hair.'

'From Brutus, my friend Maisie's cat.'

'Brutus?'

'Don't ask.'

Sarah looked closer. 'Is that dried blood matting them together?'

'Yes, and if we're right, it belongs to the person who planted the bomb.'

'How..? I mean, what on Earth led you to that discovery?'

Daisy filled her in with the previous night's events, and the possible scenario that might end up being the breakthrough. Sarah shook her head, not the least because of what she was being asked to do.

'So you want me to send this to the lab, get it DNA analysed, and avoid anyone else knowing?'

'You can get a DNA match from dried blood, can't you?'

'Yes, up to ten years after, but...'

49

Daisy squeezed her arm. 'Well then, dear... game on, I think.'

'*Daisy!* Even if I can do it in secret, I'll get shot at dawn if Burrows finds out.'

'It's only for a couple of days, Sarah. Just while we carry out our own investigation.'

'And what does that investigation entail, exactly? You're scaring me now.'

'Oh, not much, dear. But to begin with, tomorrow I'm going to see the man I think is responsible.'

'Daisy! Are you crazy?'

'Very likely. But that particular person is also responsible for what happened three years ago, so I'm asking for your understanding.'

Sarah turned away, looked out of the window across the garden. 'Celia. You still haven't told me what happened.'

Daisy joined her at the window. 'No, I know. And it's not for the right here, right now. But I'm pleading for your... discretion on this one, Sarah. Can you send the sample off to the lab, and label it so the results come back only to you?'

'I don't... well, yes I can. But there's no guarantee Burrows won't see... oh hell...'

'Thank you, Sarah,' Daisy smiled.

Sarah threw a resigned hand in the air. 'It'll take at least twenty-four hours, depending on how busy they are.'

'That's fine. And if Burrows finds out, I'll tell him I held a gun at your throat.'

'I think you already have, metaphorically at least.'

The morning wore on towards lunchtime. Daisy put in her request to HMP for a visiting order, and then took Aidan a coffee. He was busy sanding down the garage doors,

50

ready to give them a fresh coat of paint and conceal the horror of two days ago.

She left him to it. There was something she needed to do, and foraged at the back of the cloaks cupboard to find what she needed. Then she spread a sheet of newspaper on the island top, and went to work giving them a service.

They hadn't even seen the light of day for years, and she'd decided it might help her state of mind if they did.

Aidan wandered back through the kitchen door as lunchtime approached. He caught sight of Daisy carefully oiling the wheels with a little three-in-one, and grinned. A little nervously, it has to be said.

'You have got to be kidding me.'

'Dear, I don't have my dolly-trolley anymore, remember?'

'But... roller skates?'

'Yes dear. I still have them.'

'From thirty years ago.'

'Is that your politically-correct way of saying I'm too old? Anyway, it's not been thirty years. More like twenty-five.'

He shook his head. 'You'll never stay upright.'

'Course I will... with a little practice. Anyway, roller skates are all the rage now, I hear.'

'For kids, maybe.'

'Not at all. Why, there was a piece on Look East just the other day, about a granny who'd taken up roller skating.'

'Ok, I give up.'

'So you should. Now just make me a nice lunch, and then after we've eaten I'll get rolling.'

'That's what I'm afraid of.'

Daisy did get rolling. After forcing herself to remember how to strap the skates on, she wobbled her way to the kitchen door, with Aidan as the rod to her orchid.

'It's ok now, dear. I've got my legs. Well, my wheels.'

'I really don't think this is your best idea, Daisy.'

'Oh, stop being such an old fogie. I need the exercise, and anyway, I hear the Kings Lynn Roller Derby team is looking for new members.'

'God help us all.'

Daisy wasn't listening. She was already on the step, about to do or die. She pushed herself away from her rod, and managed to stay upright for the first six feet.

'Dear...'

Aidan's warning came a moment too late. The smooth concrete step gave way to the less-than-smooth drive, and Daisy got a faceful of gravel. She turned herself so she was sitting on her butt, waved an annoyed hand at Aidan.

'Why didn't you tell me small wheels and gravel don't mix?'

'I was just about...'

'Help me up, please.'

She held out a hand, spat out a few stones, and stomped her very unfeminine way to the pedestrian gate, with his arm around her for support.

'Ah, now you see... the pavement is nice and smooth.'

'Flower, are you really going to inflict yourself on public spaces?

'Well obviously I can't exactly roll in the garden, can I? Unless I want to make myself giddy pirouetting on the terrace!'

'I really don't think this is your best idea, Daisy,' Aidan reiterated, just in case she hadn't heard the first time.

Again she wasn't listening, and pushed away from him, grasping the overhanging branches of their trees as she struggled her way slightly uphill along the pathway towards the main road.

'See, Dip? I can stay upright, ye of little faith.'

'Try letting go of the branches, see what happens then.'

The moment he'd said that, Aidan groaned to himself. It sounded like the kind of challenge Daisy had never been able to resist. He already knew what was likely to happen, and she was going to do everything she could to prove it wouldn't happen.

He watched her turn hesitantly round, a determined but unsure grin set like concrete on her face. He looked down at the pavement, and realised that coming back to him she would be rolling on a downhill gradient. Then he groaned again, but reassured himself that within a few feet of letting go she would be safely on her butt.

Daisy let go of the trees, pushed off with her legs to emphasise the point. She didn't drop safely on her butt. The gradient and the determined grin gave her instant impetus, and before Aidan knew it she was heading right at him, her out of control legs slightly bent like a downhill ski racer without ski-poles.

He instinctively moved out of her way, intending to grab her to stop her going any further. He missed. It had all happened so fast, he wasn't ready. He started to run after her, but instantly realised she was already travelling far too fast for his elderly legs.

He heard her frantic cry. *'Aidaaan...'*

Then he heard the frantic cry come to an abrupt stop. He saw her reach the entrance of the pedestrian alleyway that came out onto Walcotts Lane.

And he saw the collision, as she crashed right into someone who had just walked out of the alley.

Chapter 10

The two bodies sat up, and disentangled their arms and legs. Both of them looked somewhat dishevelled, and one of them *really* didn't look happy.

'*Daisy Morrow!* You complete… moron.'

'Thank you for being my brake, Matilda,' Daisy grinned.

'*What?*'

'I don't know where I would have ended up if you hadn't come along.'

'*What?*' The fire-breathing dragon grabbed her shopping bag, clutched it to her chest like it would give her some kind of protection. '*Roller skates?* Whatever next?'

'I don't have my mobility scooter anymore, as I'm sure you know.'

'You're a disgrace, Daisy Morrow,' Matilda spluttered. 'How can someone on roller skates possibly need a mobility scooter? You're a disgraceful fraud, woman. And I'll make sure the parish council knows about it.'

Daisy looked genuinely offended. 'I paid for it, didn't get it on some kind of disabled grant.'

'You're disabled alright… in the head. I don't know, you've brought nothing but trouble ever since you moved into the village.'

'Oh come on, Matilda. That's not fair. I didn't bring any trouble for the first year.'

'Oh, that's alright then. My mistake.' She struggled to her feet, patted the dust from her coat. 'Not.'

'And just for the parish council record, I didn't actually *bring* any trouble. It was already here, I just exposed it.'

'And I suppose someone getting blown to bits in your garden isn't bringing trouble?'

Daisy's face clouded over. 'Ok, I'll give you that one. My bad. But I'm going to sort it.'

'That's what I'm afraid of.'

'Why does everyone keep saying that?'

Matilda started to stomp away, heading back home to change her coat for a clean one. Daisy called after her. 'I'm sorry, Matilda. I'll try and be a good resident from now on.'

She muttered something full of derogatory expletives, but was already striding down the alley, so fortunately Daisy couldn't hear what it was.

Then Aidan was looking down on her, still sitting on her butt. She glared at him. 'I noticed you were conspicuous by your absence. I could have done with a bit of back-up there.'

He grinned. 'Just keeping out of the way while the main cat-fight event was taking place, dear.'

She matched his grin. 'Anyway... see, I told you I could roll.'

'Hmm... maybe now you should learn how to stop.'

'I did stop.'

'Sure, with a little help from a dragon.'

'Now you're just splitting hairs.'

'I suppose one day I'll get the better of you verbally.'

'No chance. Um... dear?'

'Yes dear?' he asked, knowing exactly what she wanted.

'Could you... um... help me up, please?'

He held out a hand and helped her up onto her wobbly wheels, and then slipped an arm around her waist and virtually carried her back to the kitchen. He brushed her down on the step with the yard broom, and then she headed straight for the alcohol cupboard and poured herself a large brandy.

'I know it's only mid-afternoon, but after colliding with a fire-breathing dragon I need this.'

He grinned, flicked on the kettle to make himself a coffee, and five minutes later went back outside to finish painting the garage doors.

Alone, Daisy headed to the office, woke the PC, and pulled up her mail. She smiled as her eyes fell on the one she wanted to see. HMP had come good, and granted her an emergency visit as Roland Spence's legal council representative.

They would inform him his brief was coming to see him, of course. There was a possibility he would refuse the visit, but she knew he wouldn't. His curiosity would get the better of him. He'd want to know what was going on, and the only way to do that was to meet the person who had asked for the visit.

Daisy smiled again, but the smile held more than a little fear and uncertainty. Roland Spence was the man responsible for the emotional grief of three years ago, and she was pretty sure he was responsible for the tragedy of three days ago.

But looking at his smarmy face tomorrow, with only a prison table between them, was an ordeal she wasn't exactly looking forward to.

Chapter 11

Aidan wandered into the bedroom and found Daisy sitting at the dressing table, brushing her long dark brown locks carefully. She heard the giggle he tried to muffle, and turned round.

'Something funny, dear?'

'You look… like you're wearing a wig, dear.'

'That's because I am… which your galactic brain has clearly worked out.'

'That's not going to fool Spence for long.'

'I don't want it to. Just long enough for me to sit down alone with him will be long enough. Then he'll take a closer look and realise who I am.'

'You really do have a wicked side.'

'Where he's concerned I'd take the rifle if I could.'

'Maybe a good job you can't then.'

'That's a matter of opinion.'

She stood up, gave him a twirl. He let out an admiring whistle. The close fitting dark-blue trouser suit hugged the trim shape she'd never lost, and make her look every bit the part of a power-dressing legal eagle.

'Most impressive. I'd have you as my brief… even without the wig.'

'Now you're just trying to flatter me. I've booked us in at the Park Plaza, so we can make a night of it. I might need a cocktail or two after seeing that piece of shit.'

'Our overnight bag is packed and ready.'

'Perhaps time we got to the station then.'

They headed downstairs. Then the crunch of tyres on the drive filled their ears. 'No prizes for guessing who that is.'

Sarah walked through the kitchen door and stopped in her tracks. 'Wow... Winona Ryder eat your heart out!'

'Now *you're* flattering me. So do I need to ask what you're doing here?'

'I'm coming with you,' Sarah announced, like it was a surprise to either of them.

'*Me and my big mouth...* again,' Daisy whispered. Then, a little louder, 'In your uniform?'

'Yes. I thought it might give your little subterfuge a bit more kudos if you turned up with an officer of the law.'

Aidan looked at Daisy. 'Can't argue with that, dear.'

Daisy sighed, knowing he was right. 'You make a good point, Sarah. But Aidan and me are staying overnight. I suppose the Plaza will have a spare room though.'

'Oh no, I'll head back to Norfolk when we're done with Spence. There just might be some news from the lab later.'

They headed to Sarah's car, and sank into the seats. Daisy glanced over to Sarah. 'So is this an official accompaniment?'

'Hell no. It's my day off, and if Burrows finds out I'm wearing my uniform off duty I really will be shot.'

A two-hour train ride took them to Liverpool Street station. Then another fifteen minutes underground ride on the Waterloo line took them to Waterloo station. A five minute walk past the London Eye, and they were walking through the revolving doors of the Park Plaza, and signing in at reception.

Daisy looked longingly across to the cocktail bar, but resisted the temptation for a little Dutch courage, helped by a steer-away arm from Aidan. It didn't stop her flicking on the kettle as soon as they walked in the room, and tearing open two sticks of Nescafe for her mug.

They had an hour before Daisy and Sarah would have to leave, so Daisy stretched out on the bed, took off her shoes.

'Is there anything I should know about three years ago, before I come face to face with him?' Sarah asked.

'No, my dear. If it's ok, I'll do the talking. You're just there to look pretty this time.'

'So if everything works out well, I guess the next time I see Roland Spence it won't be so pretty?'

'Let's hope so. But you'll have to get behind me in the queue, trust me.'

'Now I'm quaking in my boots.'

Daisy just nodded, unwilling to let on she was quaking in her boots too.

They walked together the quarter-mile back to Waterloo station. Aidan had promised to play nicely, go for a long walk along the Thames and a trip on the London Eye, and Daisy had hugged him a little tighter than usual before they parted.

They boarded the train to Plumstead, and thirty minutes later found themselves on the station forecourt in the early afternoon sunshine.

'Shall we get a taxi?' said Sarah

'My dear, if you don't mind, I'd like to walk. Get a little fresh air before getting suffocated in Spence's company.'

'Fine by me.'

They walked arm-in-arm, Daisy's face growing grimmer with every passing yard, and then the high forbidding walls of the prison were there in front of them.

'You sure you're up to this, Daisy?'

'No, but I have to be. Let's go get it over with.'

The officer at visitor reception looked at them a little curiously, but then Daisy switched on a false smile and handed him the visiting order she'd printed off, with the business card pinned to it that was many years old, and spoke in clipped English tones.

'Flora Bundy, here to see Roland Spence. I'm his new legal representative. This is Officer Lowry, accompanying me as this is a police matter.'

'Good luck with that,' the officer replied curtly.

'I beg your pardon?' said Daisy, equally curtly.

The officer looked up, acknowledging the businesslike tone. Sara flashed her badge, as briefly as she could get away with. 'He's waiting in the interview room. I'll get someone to take you.'

'Please do. And quickly, if you don't mind. The law waits for no man.'

He shook his head. 'I'll need to see your briefcase.'

Daisy handed it over with a huff. He opened it up, saw there was nothing inside but papers, and handed it back. Two wardens appeared from nowhere, asked that they accompany them, and the fake legal brief and her unofficial police companion followed them along stark corridors.

'Wow, this place is depressing,' said Sarah as they walked.

'Not depressing enough for him.'

Sarah threw her a warning stare. 'Just keep a lid on it, ok?'

Daisy smiled sweetly. 'Don't worry dear... I've got you to protect me from him.'

'Actually, I think I'm here more to protect him from you.'

The wardens unlocked the final gate, and then the peeling paint of the door to the interview room was in front

61

of them. 'He's in there,' said one of them. 'You can go in. We'll wait out here in case you need us.'

Daisy nodded, and swallowed hard without it trying to look like she was. One of the wardens unlocked the door, and she switched into businesslike mode and pushed it open firmly.

But she'd only taken a few steps into the room when she realised her disguise was maybe not as good as she'd thought. Roland Spence was sitting calmly, his wrists chained to the table in the centre of the room.

He *was* sitting calmly, until he set eyes on the two women who had walked in. His eyes grew wide, his body looked like it had just experienced the electric chair.

'*You...*' he gasped.

Chapter 12

Daisy's heart sank, mostly because she'd been denied the opportunity of sitting down with him for a minute or two before he sussed out who she was. It didn't really matter, but it was a little bit of one-upmanship she wasn't going to get to enjoy. Twelve years in prison obviously hadn't dimmed his sharp mind.

But then she focussed on his eyes, and realised his disbelieving stare wasn't aimed at her.

He was looking at Sarah.

Sarah glanced nervously to Daisy, already realising why he'd reacted the way he had. And Daisy knew it too. It sent a stab of pain right through her heart, froze her brain inside her skull for a moment. She swallowed hard, instantly composed herself. She had to; the events of three years ago had suddenly been ripped into the present, but it wasn't the main reason she was there.

They took their seats on the opposite side of the metal desk, and Daisy slapped her briefcase onto the top, making as much deliberate noise as she could.

But Roland Spence still wasn't looking at her. He peered closer at Sarah, and then leant back a little, looked more relaxed.

'*It isn't you, is it,*' he said, almost to himself.

Daisy knew exactly who he'd thought it was, but right then she had no intention of revealing the fact she did. 'Mr. Spence, I'm Flora Bundy. I've been assigned to your case. This is Officer Lowry, the liaison officer handling this case.'

He finally switched his gaze to Daisy, ran a hand through his rich bad-boy dark-brown locks. Prison hadn't changed his appearance much; Daisy had half-expected his hair to be cropped, his features drawn and pale. She'd kind of hoped for it too.

But the flowing, rich-kid locks of his early forties were still there, the dark eyes still pierced into her from chestnut, manicured eyebrows, and his olive-toned skin wasn't exactly wrapping tightly around prominent high cheekbones.

She felt somewhat disappointed prison life seemed to be agreeing with him. Then again, people like him always somehow managed to get the best out of any situation.

It was everyone else who ended up suffering.

He grinned at her in the supercilious, superior way he grinned at everyone. 'I'm curious, Flora Bundy. Your visit is a little surprising... and even more so because it would appear a case of shutting the stable door after the horse has bolted, as they say in the country.'

The grin never faded, and the clipped, English posh-but-not-posh intonation he'd always adopted sent a shiver down her spine. She didn't show it. 'Mr. Spence, new information has come to light.'

'Oh, really?'

'Yes. Information that may implicate you in further crimes, and has the potential to increase your time in prison.'

'I see.' He sat back, and Daisy saw his fists clench momentarily. She'd scored a minor victory, making him think for a second or two that the new information might be good news. He didn't flinch for long.

'So, Miss Bundy... it is *Miss* I take it?'

'It is.'

'Not surprising,' he looked pleased at his own joke. 'Miss Bundy, are you suggesting that I might have been partaking

64

in criminal activities, even though I've been in prison for the last twelve years?'

The urge to reach over and thump him was almost too much to bear, but Daisy managed to resist, smiled sweetly instead. 'I think we both know a little thing like being locked up isn't going to stop you from organising illegal activities, Mr. Spence.'

He feigned a look of shock. 'Miss Bundy, please... are you the solicitor for the prosecution or the defence?'

'I'm your brief, Mr. Spence. But if I'm going to represent you, it needs to be told like it is; between us at least.'

He leant back and crossed his legs, shook his head. 'I see there are no flies on you, Miss... Bundy. Pray tell, what is it I am supposed to have done now?'

'There has been an allegation made that you were instrumental in ordering a hit on someone, which took place three days ago.'

He narrowed his eyes and shook his head, making a lock of his dark hair fall across his left eye in a menacing kind of way. 'And was I successful in this alleged *hit*, Miss Bundy?'

Daisy tried to ignore the lock of hair, fixed her stare into his. 'It appears an innocent man lost his life, but the person who was the actual target wasn't harmed.'

'That's a pity.'

'I'm sorry?'

'I meant, it's a pity an innocent man lost his life. Please give the family my commiserations.'

'Really.'

'Yes, really. I'm not that inhuman, despite my reputation.'

'Glad to hear it. So, I'm here to take a statement of your innocence of the allegations, Mr. Spence.'

'Really.'

'Yes, really.'

'So you're not here investigating your own attempted murder, Daisy Henderson?'

Chapter 13

She hadn't fooled him for a minute. Not that she really expected to, but she'd hoped to be the one to reveal her true identity at the point she chose. He'd forced the issue, so there was no choice now but to run with it.

'I see you're just as sharp as ever, Roland.'

'That wig looks idiotic, Daisy.'

'Maybe... but it got me to you, dear boy.'

He flicked back his head, sending the menacing lock of hair away from his eyes, much to Daisy's relief. 'So why are you here, Mrs. Henderson? I assume you are not asking me to star in a production at the theatre you just bought?'

'Very funny. But I might present you with a murder charge instead.'

'Good luck with that.'

Daisy leant forward, her elbows on the table either side of the briefcase. His dismissive attitude was firing up her spirit, and she knew she had to do something to wipe the smile off his face.

'I don't need luck, Roland. There's something in this briefcase that will help to bring the justice you deserve.'

For a fleeting moment he looked unsure. It didn't last long. The sickly smile was back. 'As I said, old woman... good luck with that.'

The urge to thump him was back, but instead Daisy stood the briefcase up on the table, and turned it so one edge was pointing at the prisoner. Slowly she undid the top, slipped her hand inside. 'As I said, Mr. Spence, I don't need luck...'

Sarah, who had stayed silent up to then, realised what was happening and started to play the game. 'I really don't think you should, Daisy. It's not worth it...'

Roland Spence finally looked like a rabbit caught in headlights. 'Oh, come on... you'd never have got a weapon through inspection...'

Daisy knew she'd got him right where she wanted. 'You're not the only one with friends in the prison service, Roland,' she said sweetly.

Suddenly he was stammering. 'Look... you really don't want to do anything rash... they'll arrest you...'

'Of course they will. But as you said, dear boy, I'm an old woman now, so what happens to me isn't as important as justice...'

'Daisy... look... I know I swore revenge when you first locked me up. But I got it, didn't I?'

Daisy stopped rummaging in the almost-empty briefcase, but kept her hand on the imaginary gun. 'So what are you saying, Roland?'

'Please take your hand out of that case.'

'If you tell me the truth.'

'Ok... I promise.'

'You promise?'

'Fair point. But I'll tell you what I know. Prom... well, you know.'

Daisy slowly withdrew her hand from the case, but left it pointing at the prisoner. 'It's cocked and ready, Roland. Neither you or anyone else will stop me, if I deem it necessary.'

He sat back, but both feet stayed firmly on the floor, one of them tapping out a nervous rhythm. 'Sure... I didn't mean the *old woman* bit, you know that, right?'

'Just tell me what I want to hear.'

He tried to throw his hands in the air, but the chains stopped him. 'Look Daisy... I don't think this is what you want to hear, but I saw the news reports. I know what happened three days ago. But I swear it was nothing to do with me.'

'I don't believe you.' Daisy reached out a hand towards the briefcase.

'Please... on my mother's life... whatever... it wasn't me.'

Daisy took the hand away again. 'So you are telling us you had nothing to do with ordering the hit?'

He shook his head rapidly from side to side, making the lock of hair fall across his eye again. But this time it didn't seem anywhere near as menacing. 'Nothing. It wasn't me. Honestly.'

'*Honestly?*'

'Ok, bad choice of word. But I don't know what other word I can use to convince you not to shoot me.'

'So that's what this is about? You'd say anything so I won't pull the trigger?' The hand headed to the bag again.

'Yes... no... you're putting words in my mouth now.'

'Ok, I won't shoot you. Yet. So tell me again without looking like a frightened hare.'

He leant forward, fixed his eyes into Daisy's. 'It wasn't me. And I'm really sorry... really... but I have no idea who it was.'

Daisy sat back, allowed the hand to settle onto her lap. 'Second matter... what was that all about when you first set eyes on Officer Lowry?'

'You know what it was all about.'

'I'm asking you. What do you know that I don't?'

'I don't actually know what you know, do I?'

'Stop being pedantic. I'm still happy to get *persuasive*, and you know exactly why.'

69

He nodded his head. 'Look Daisy, you and I have history. Back in the day when you were with MI6 I resented you for getting me put away. I swore revenge in the courtroom, remember?'

'How could I forget? The look you gave me was pure evil.'

'Yes, well, back then I was pure evil. No one got in my way and came out smelling of roses. It took me a while to find out how to get the best out of prison life... how to manipulate people, if you understand me. For a few years I concentrated on building the prison dream. But the desire to get even with you never diminished.'

'So why target Celia? She was innocent.'

He lowered his head. 'You want the truth, Daisy? It doesn't make easy listening.'

Daisy lowered her head too, a sudden sadness overcoming the will to kill the man responsible, before he told the truth anyway. 'You never told me the truth three years ago. You kept it all locked away, deliberately. Why should I believe you want to tell all now?'

'Maybe because you came here to kill me?' He caught the look. 'Ok... if you must know, the last three years have changed me. Well, *modified* me, maybe. I doubt I'll ever change my fundamental beliefs.'

'Take what you want, and believe you're superior to everyone else you mean?'

'Something like that, yes.'

'You're a sad man. So how have you got *modified*?'

'Maybe because I realised no matter how superior I am, I'm still vulnerable to people who want to take me down. As I get older I begin to wonder if it's all worth it.'

'That's astonishing, coming from you.'

'How do you think I felt, actually thinking it?'

70

'So how does that relate to the here and now?'

'You've suffered enough retribution. So now I want to tell you what I know about your daughter. But I have to warn you, it still won't give you closure.'

Chapter 14

Daisy hesitated. She was getting what she wanted, but suddenly if felt like she wasn't so sure she did want to know anymore. But rather like jumping off a cliff, she'd made the leap and now there was no way to avoid hitting the ground.

'Tell me what you know.'

'You're not going to kill me?'

'That depends on what you have to tell me.'

'That's not fair. I need a guarantee I'll stay living.'

Daisy looked into his eyes. They seemed like he knew for certain how perilous he believed his situation to be. Like he meant it when he said he would tell her what he knew, and be truthful about it.

'Ok, Roland. I'll not shoot you. But the gun stays cocked.'

He nodded meekly. 'The Celia incident was a complete cock-up. I was stuck in here, so I had to rely on others to carry out my orders. Sadly for me, those others had their own agenda.'

'I take it you're referring to Jason Briggs?'

'Him and his nasty Nigerian sidekick Adde, yes.'

'Go on.'

'I wanted you dead... sorry Daisy. But Briggs apparently decided killing you was too risky for him, so went after your daughter instead. I told him I wasn't happy about that, but, well, he was a free man and I wasn't. I couldn't stop him doing his worst...'

'*Please don't say it,*' Daisy whispered.

'You need to hear this, even though it's not the whole story. What I didn't know at the time was that he was running a lucrative sideline in illegal immigration. I don't think he killed your daughter, Daisy, but...'

72

'But what?'

'It seems he brought immigrants in through the container ports, using containers which then went back where they'd come from. But not totally empty.'

'Are you telling me...'

'Apparently he'd tapped into a two-way market, discovered that beautiful English girls could fetch a high price from rich Middle-Eastern and African men who wanted a trophy on their arm.

'Are you talking about a reverse modern day slavery racket?'

'I'm afraid so, yes. As you know, Briggs got caught by the Metropolitan Police soon after the Celia incident, squealed like a frightened rat and implicated me in your daughter's abduction. Added a few years on my sentence, the bastard. But right after he was caught, his crew shut down the immigration operation, totally and instantly. The police never found any evidence it had ever existed.'

'That explains why I never knew either.'

For a second he looked genuinely regretful. 'I'm sorry, Daisy. Please believe me, I didn't want any of that. Drugs and arms trading, they're fair game for me. But abducting innocent young women... that's not on. But don't you see? Going after you bent on revenge just ended up getting me a longer sentence. I learnt my lesson, and I have to live with your daughter getting the rough end of Brigg's nature instead.'

'So why the hell didn't you tell me all this three years ago?'

He shook his head like he really didn't know. 'Raging bitterness, I suppose. You'd suffered a horrible event, and as I saw it back then, indirectly you'd been responsible for me doing more time. But as the months passed, I began to realise it wasn't your doing, even though I was trying to tell myself it was. It took me two years to get over the bitterness, and accept it was Briggs who was the one really at fault.'

'He died in prison a year ago, I understand?'

'Yeah. Someone took a dislike to his ugly face and his even uglier attitude, and stuck a shard of glass in him. Jolly good riddance if you ask me.'

'I agree with you there. So... so what happened to Celia? Where is she?' The voice was small, reluctant to ask the question.

He shook his head again. 'I really wish I could tell you. All I know is Briggs shipped her out the day before he was arrested. She could be anywhere now... but it will be a long way from here.'

Daisy blinked away the mistiness, determined not to show Roland Spence his words had got to her. Under the desk, Sarah slipped a hand into hers.

Daisy's words were spoken quietly. 'I suppose I should thank you for finally coming clean. I just wish you'd done it three years ago.'

'In all honesty I would have told you a year ago, but I wasn't prepared to face your wrath. Now you forced me to face it anyway.'

'I can understand that.'

'So if I may ask, what happens now?'

Daisy stood up. 'Nothing. Just go about running Belmarsh as you've done up to now. But just be aware, if I find any evidence that might implicate you further, I won't hesitate to make sure it gets to the right channels. Do I make myself clear?

He nodded meekly.

'And thank you, Mr. Spence, for telling me what I needed to know. Well, a little more than I expected, actually. Perhaps it will go some way to lifting a weight from your shoulders. Come along, Officer Lowry...'

She picked the briefcase off the table, showed him the inside. 'And just so you know, there never was a weapon, dear boy.'

The late afternoon sunshine made them both squint as the heavy main door of the prison closed behind them. Daisy pulled the phone from her pocket, called a taxi.

'I'm sure as hell not walking to Plumstead station, not after that,' she growled.

'Daisy...'

'Sarah dear, forgive me but it's perhaps not a good idea to involve me in conversation and sympathy right now. There's a little too much to think about.'

Sarah nodded, deciding her friend was right. Roland Spence had for sure given her an awful lot to get her head and her heart around.

Chapter 15

Daisy sipped her Sazerak cocktail in the bar at the Park Plaza, a concerned-looking Aidan as close by her side as he could get.

'Dear, at the end of the day, Roland Spence gave you some information, even though it maybe wasn't what you were expecting. You should see the day as a success.'

'I was convinced it was him.'

'And now you don't think it was?'

Daisy took another gulp of the cocktail, her eyes fixed through the window to the taxis and buses speeding round the oval-shaped hotel on the other side of the street. She wasn't seeing them, or anything else, Spence's words thumping around her head with such force they were blocking out everything else.

An hour ago they'd said a quiet goodbye to Sarah in the hotel lobby. Daisy had hugged her tightly, apologised for her stunned silence and the virtual lack of conversation since they'd left the prison. Sarah seemed to understand, even though she didn't know anywhere near the full story of Celia's disappearance.

But Roland Spence's words had filled in a few blanks that neither she nor Daisy knew, and Sarah was getting to know her new friend well enough to understand she needed space to come to terms with what she'd suddenly been told. They parted company, and Sarah said she'd call later in the evening when she'd got home.

As soon as she'd gone Daisy had dragged Aidan into the cocktail bar, and was on her third cocktail in less than an hour. She turned her sad eyes away from the window, smiled to him and took his hand.

'It wasn't Spence, dear. I know that for sure now. But it leaves us back at square one.'

He squeezed her hand. 'Not quite square one, Flower. We now know some stuff about Celia we didn't know before.'

She nodded sadly, wiped away a sudden tear. 'Yes, we do. I wasn't expecting him to gush quite as much as he did, and it's kind of stunned me.'

'Prison changes people, dear.'

'Yes, usually for the worse.'

He grinned ruefully. 'Age changes people too... well, some people.'

'What are you saying, dear?'

He chuckled. 'Nothing. Well, just that the fact you don't seem to have changed much in the last twenty years was the impetus for you to take it on yourself to go see Spence.'

'And where has that got me, Dip?'

The words were spoken with a hint of anger. He put an arm around her shoulder, pulled them together. 'When you get your head around it, you'll see that it's got us somewhere. Ok, he wasn't responsible for the hit on you, and you are correct, we are back to square one on that. But when it comes to Celia, he's told us more than we knew before. No matter how dreadful her scenario is, at least it's a new scenario. It's likely she's not dead now. And yes, I'm telling it like it is, harsh and blunt as it may be.'

Daisy rested her head against his shoulder, smiled at his harsh bluntness. 'You've always been my rock, dear. Your wise words have kept me on the... kind of straight and narrow, when all my impetuous side wanted to do was fire off somewhere else. What would I do without you?'

'Be a damn site more impetuous than you already are?'

77

'For sure. But the thing that keeps thumping around my head is that our daughter is out there somewhere, likely going through hell… and she could be anywhere in the world.'

'So now we start looking for her, and stop looking for her body.'

'Blunt again, dear. But how do we go about it? Roland has answered one question, but given us a hundred new ones.'

'I can't argue with that. The man who went against Spence's wishes and trafficked Celia, Jason Briggs, is dead. The police never even knew he was running a secret trafficking operation, and his crew immediately shut it down right after he was arrested, never to be seen again. And all that was three years ago.'

'Doesn't leave us much to go on, does it?'

He shook his head. 'I suppose we could try and find out who his associates were at that time?'

Daisy shook her head. 'Maybe. But do you really think they're going to talk and implicate themselves in the process… even if they remember one individual girl from three years ago?'

'Probably not. But right now shall we go eat? My long walk earlier has left me starving!'

Surprisingly, Daisy found herself quite hungry too, even though she'd told her head she couldn't stomach a thing. As they ate in the hotel's high-ceilinged restaurant, she began to feel more like herself. The food was good, Aidan had deliberately kept away from delicate subjects, and bit by bit her spirit came back to life.

Inevitably though, the subject had to come up. 'The news about Celia doesn't change one thing though.'

78

He glanced up, knowing exactly what she meant. 'Whoever wanted you dead is still wanting you dead.'

She grinned at his bluntness, yet again. 'You have such a way with words, dear. It doesn't stop you being right though. We still have to find out who killed Bob, before we do anything else.'

'You think it was one of the other two names you gave Burrows?'

'Possibly. I'll have to ask Sarah tomorrow when she's back at the station, see if there's been any developments on that.'

'But you're not holding out much hope?'

'Roland Spence rather took the wind from my sails, dear. I think we have to regroup, start thinking in a different way. But right now, I want to finish enjoying my night away!'

He nodded his agreement. They went back to enjoying the nicely-cooked food, but not for long. Five minutes later Daisy's phone started jumping around on the table. She picked it up, looked at it curiously. 'It's Sarah. She's a bit early... hello, Sarah. You can't be back home already, surely?'

The voice on the other end sounded excited, but that was nothing unusual. *'Hi Daisy. No, I'm still on the train. But I just got a call from my friend at the lab. They got a match from the dried blood.'*

Daisy raised her eyebrows, flicked the phone to speaker. 'Well, I have to confess half of me is shocked it worked. Go on.'

'Well, don't get too excited yet. I need to get to the station tomorrow, do some digging. But he's on our database, according to the lab.'

'Sounds promising. Are you going to tell us who it is, or carry on being infuriating?'

They heard her laugh. *'Sorry. The name on the database is Adde Wambua, He's Nigerian apparently. Ring any bells?'*

It did ring a bell. The first name, anyway. 'Roland Spence mentioned someone called Adde, said he was Nigerian. Jason Briggs' ex-partner, apparently.'

'Yeah. Bit of a coincidence, don't you think?'

'It is a coincidence. But it doesn't explain why he would want me dead after all this time. He might be a lead to finding Celia though.'

'Ok Daisy. Just wanted to give you the news. Let me call you tomorrow, when I've had chance to dig a bit. We'll know more for sure then.'

Daisy ended the call, glanced to Aidan. 'What do you think about that then, dear?'

He narrowed his eyes. 'The plot thickens...'

Chapter 16

The train ride home the next morning was made in the rain. Daisy and Aidan spent the two hours huddled together over the table in the first-class carriage, trying to work out what their next move was.

There wasn't much to go on. Until Sarah did her stuff and discovered more about the thug in question, there was little they could plan. Her call couldn't come soon enough for Daisy, the frustration of a lack of knowledge building inside her the closer they got to Norwich.

'It's almost lunchtime. Why hasn't she called yet?'

'Relax, Flower. You asked her to keep her findings to herself for now, remember? It might be taking time to do things she's not supposed to?'

'I guess. Maybe another paper cup of coffee?'

The weather wasn't any better once they got to Norwich. Jumping on the connection to Kings Lynn they were protected from the rain by the large concourse roof, but as soon as the train left the station, the wind buffeted the side of the carriage with huge raindrops.

After they'd grabbed a taxi at Kings Lynn and made the final leg to Great Wiltingham, the drive at the cottage was a soggy mess of puddles. Some of the black and yellow tape was still draped around the front gate, a sudden and sickening reminder of what had taken place there a few days previously.

Daisy headed straight for the brandy, poured them both a glass. 'Don't worry dear, it's just the one,' she reassured Aidan.

It wasn't difficult to see she wasn't in the best of moods, and he knew exactly why. The previous day she'd got a faceful of facts from Roland Spence she hadn't expected. One of them was that he'd had nothing to do with the attempt on her life. She'd not expected that; quite the opposite in fact. She'd convinced herself that meeting him would have confirmed he was the man responsible, and it would have been a simple matter to then let the police deal with it.

That hadn't happened, and the quick, clean resolution had been anything but. Back to square one didn't really cover it... now whoever wanted her dead was still out there and free, and could try again at any moment.

It wasn't a nice place for her to be.

But it was even worse than that. What he had told her had reopened old wounds, and shed a torch of new light onto them. A new light that was no less soothing, and had ended up raising yet more questions.

Their daughter was very likely still alive, but also very likely living through hell. He knew all too well they'd both started to believe Celia was dead; the search for her was more the search for her body.

From now on, that search would be different. And even harder. Now they were going to have to seek her believing she was alive... and do so in a vastly bigger area.

That wasn't a nice place for Daisy to be either.

He made her the comfort food of cheese on toast with added pepperoni and jalapenos. It stood little chance of bringing her any comfort, but he had to try something. She disappeared into the bedroom, removed the dark wig, and at least looked more herself, even if it was just a physical thing.

Then, at three in the afternoon, her phone rang.

'You took your time... oh, sorry Sarah. Afraid I'm a bit screwed up at the moment.'

'It's ok. Have a go at me if it helps.'

Daisy wiped away a tear. 'No, it doesn't. And it isn't... ok I mean. You of all people are going above and beyond. We really appreciate it, even if I don't always make that clear.'

'It really is ok, Daisy. I had to wait until Burrows was otherwise engaged before I delved into people I wasn't supposed to know about, And when I did, I didn't get a lot of anything useful, sad to say.'

Daisy closed her eyes, feeling her heart sink to the floor. 'Tell me what you did find.'

'He's got a rap list as long as your arm, a real piece of work. When Briggs was arrested they got him too, but not for the trafficking side of things, as you probably guessed. He kept quiet about that, but squealed like a strangled cat about everything else in order to get a shorter sentence.'

'Whatever happened to honour amongst thieves, huh?'

I think that went out with pistols at dawn, Daisy. Anyway, he was out of prison after six months...'

'And back to his old dishonourable ways, I guess?'

'Probably.'

'What does *probably* mean?'

'After he got out of prison he went off the radar. The police haven't seen sight nor sound of him for over two years.'

'Please don't tell me he's a reformed character too?'

'Doubt it. But he's doing whatever he's doing without us knowing about it. Not so much as a parking ticket.'

'Bugger, as Aidan is just about to say. Sarah, please come for dinner when you're done there, let me say sorry for being a bitch.'

'I told you, there's no need to say sorry. But I'll come anyway. About six-thirty?'

Daisy killed the call, told Aidan the lack of news. 'Seems we really are back to square one, dear. Clearly Adde Wambua or whoever he's working for wants me dead for some unfathomable reason, but we don't know the who or the why. Sarah's coming for dinner later, so we can barnstorm what we've got then. But it's next to nothing, I'm afraid.'

He headed to the kitchen, to see what was in the freezer to make a suitable barnstorming-type meal.

'Bugger,' he said as he went.

Chapter 17

The barnstorming didn't exactly reveal much. Aidan's linguini with prawns went down a storm, but the barn part wasn't exactly a raising. With the murderer off the radar, there weren't a lot of roads to follow until he made an appearance again.

Daisy did everything she could to apologise to Sarah, even though it wasn't necessary, but the frustration of being told the harsh facts of life yet being unable to act on them was beginning to show on her face.

'Do you think he went back to Nigeria when he was released, then somehow slipped back into the UK without being noticed?'

Sarah nodded. 'It's a possibility. His ex-partner knew all about getting in here illegally, after all.'

'So if he was operating in another country, do you think you could find out, Sarah?'

'I could ask Interpol to check it out, but it's yet another thing I won't be doing officially, unless we bring Burrows in on it. And I don't suppose you want me to do that still, do you?'

Daisy put a hand on her arm. 'I'm so sorry. How about we keep him out of it for one more day? If we've not made any progress after that, we tell him all.'

'You really are holding that AK-47 of yours to my throat, aren't you?'

Daisy smiled ruefully. 'No, I save that for the bad guys. In your case I'm just asking nicely.'

'Knowing I won't refuse you.'

'Well...'

'One more day, that's the deal. Tomorrow I'll see if Interpol can turn anything up, but if not, then we go public. I can't do any more than that, Daisy... especially after our last adventure.'

Daisy filled her wineglass. 'I understand, dear. Thank you for understanding too.'

'Maybe one day you'll have more faith in the British police.'

Sarah waved goodbye to a slightly-forlorn Daisy and Aidan, and drove the five miles to her parents' home in East Winch. She'd just stepped out of her car when she spotted a slightly unusual sight in the road outside.

A beautiful and very valuable vintage Rolls Royce was driving slowly past. Nobody who lived in the village owned such a rare vehicle. She walked to the pavement and narrowed her eyes to try and see better. It was dark so she couldn't make out much, but she did notice a strange figure sitting in the back seat.

A woman with black hair and white highlights seemed to be dressed to match the hair, all black and white, and clearly being chauffeur-driven. She'd never seen her before, and East Winch was hardly the kind of tourist hot-spot people with her kind of money frequented.

Sarah wasn't quite sure why, but she jumped back into the car, turned onto the road and followed the Rolls a few hundred yards behind. She didn't have to drive for long. Just the other side of the village, the car turned into a brick-pillared entranceway.

Sarah drove slowly past the entrance. The car had pulled to a stop just outside the double-doored main entrance to the big old house.

86

She didn't stop, wary of being spotted. But she'd seen what she needed. She knew the house, a lot better than she really wanted to. She'd been there before, and incurred Daisy's wrath because she wasn't supposed to have been, putting herself in danger to look out for her friend.

She drove back to the annex of her parents' home where she lived, a slightly uneasy feeling in her gut that had no real reason to be there. Maybe it was just seeing Harrington Manor again; maybe just the awful memories actually seeing it brought back.

But its former owner was Finn Finnegan, the man they'd brought down three weeks previously. And now, suddenly, a strange woman was there, driving into the grounds at ten in the evening like she had every right to be there.

Sarah brewed herself a tea, and fell into bed to drink it under the cosiness of the duvet, finding her thoughts captivated by what she'd just seen. Ok, it was an unusual sight in a village like East Winch, but what was it that had made her jump back in the car and follow the Rolls Royce?

She tried to analyse her own actions, but failed dismally. It didn't make any sense; whoever was in the car had just as much right as anyone else to be driving down the main street. Just as much right to be in the village as she had.

But something felt off. Maybe it was a copper's intuition, maybe at heart she was just as nosy as half the residents in the village. But as she felt the weariness of a busy day start to take her away to dreamland, she decided she had to tell Daisy about what she'd seen, and find out what she made of it.

Chapter 18

As the new day dawned, Sarah wandered into her parents' kitchen. She had a small kitchen in her annex, but she wanted to see if her father had any more information about the strange woman in the Rolls. She found him brewing fresh coffee, and as he handed her a cup she decided to broach the subject.

'Hey dad. When I got back last night I saw an unusual sight. A vintage Rolls Royce drove past, with a very peculiar woman in it. You any idea who she was?'

He chuckled, nodded his head. 'She arrived a few days ago. She's Finn's Belgian mother, come to arrange the removal of his personal possessions before the manor is sold by order of the state, apparently. I'm surprised you don't know about that, given the police involvement.'

'We were only officially involved in the murder investigation, which was solved by Finn squealing on who killed Jesse. The drugs squad handled everything else, and they don't tell us squat.'

'Well, according to village gossip, she's a strange one for sure. Arrived in that Rolls, driven by her personal chauffeur it seems.'

'You know her name?'

'Cruella deVille, or something.'

She laughed. 'Dad, she was a character in a Disney movie. *One hundred and one Dalmatians*, remember?'

'From what I've seen, they must have based her character on Finn's mother!'

Sarah headed back to the annex to dress in her uniform. Her father's words had done nothing but make her more curious, more determined to relay the development to Daisy.

But first she had to contact Interpol, and see if the man who tried to murder her had any kind of international criminal record.

It was ten in the morning when Daisy took a stroll. The day had dawned sunny, and the pavements were steaming slightly as the sun burned off the heavy rain of the previous day. It was a lovely autumn morning, and the ducks swimming in the pond seemed to know it too, loudly quacking their innocent pleasure in the September air.

She felt a pang of envy, wished she was one of those ducks. Just for a while, it would be nice to only have to think about finding the next meal. Instead she was looking over her shoulder, wondering if the perfectly innocent figure standing at the other end of the pond was the person who wanted her dead. Listening out for any sound that would indicate her life was about to come to an end.

And just as bad as all that, she didn't have a clue where that person was, or even who he was working for.

She shook her head, and quickened her step without realising she was. A cup of coffee with Maisie, combined with her slightly-dotty take on life, sounded like a good way to force her mind away from how precarious her life was right then.

Her friend was on form. 'I was just about to take Brutus for a walk. But now you're here, we'll have a coffee first.'

'Thanks, Maisie. Think I need one.'

'Don't tell me Aidan has broken the coffee machine again?'

She grinned. 'No, Maisie. Just fancied a bit of different company, that's all.'

89

'Oh good. I must say, Brutus seems happier. You didn't give him full-cream milk, did you? I hear there's funny things in it.'

Daisy shook her head. 'Only semi-skimmed, dear. But I might know why he's happier.'

She told Maisie of the discovery, and what it had led to, and apologised for giving her cat an unauthorised haircut. Her friend didn't seem too perturbed.

'I knew he was bothered about something, but he wouldn't tell me what it was. Glad you discovered what was bugging him.'

'Me to. But it hasn't got me very far.'

'No dear, but it still might. I did try to instil a sense of right and wrong into him, you know.'

'Brutus?'

'Of course. Who else, dear? When he found that man meddling with your scooter, he knew it wasn't right.'

Daisy groaned, tried not to let it show. 'Or he got kicked in the face, and decided that definitely wasn't right.'

'Daisy!'

'Sorry. But he is a cat, Maisie.' She saw the thunderous look on her friend's face. 'A very, very intelligent one, of course.'

'You should be grateful, Daisy. My big brave Brutus has helped to solve the mystery of who is after you. Perhaps I should rename him Sherlock.'

'Oh, I am grateful, believe me. Your big, brave, hairy, super-intelligent cat has been a great help.'

'And he's good on the lead too.'

'How could I forget that?'

'Would you like to come for a walk with us, Daisy? I'm sure we'd both be delighted to have you along.'

90

'Um... thank you, Maisie, but I, um... promised Aidan I'd make him lunch.'

'That's a first, dear,' Maisie said, only slightly sarcastically.

Daisy did walk with Maisie and Brutus, but only as far as her gate. Then they waved goodbye, except for Brutus, who wasn't quite that intelligent, and she headed into the kitchen through the side door.

Aidan was fiddling with the coffee machine, and for a moment Daisy thought Maisie must have had some kind of mystic vision, but then he straightened up and she could see he was just refilling it.

He smiled a greeting. 'Sarah has just called. She's got a little news, and you might find it somewhat interesting.'

Chapter 19

Daisy got straight on the phone. What she heard didn't sound that exciting, to begin with.

'We've officially investigated the two names you gave to Burrows. One of them is dead, killed in a gang war two years ago. The other went la-la, has been in a mental institution for the last five years, and apparently doesn't even know what century it is.'

'I suppose that's no surprise. I didn't think either of them would be a suspect.'

'Of course you didn't. You only gave him those names to keep him occupied, didn't you?'

'Well...'

'Unofficially, Interpol have no record of Adde Wambua. Seems he moved to France when he got out of prison, and then disappeared completely. So no one knows his whereabouts.'

'Now I'm even more depressed. So why did Aidan say you had something interesting to tell me?'

'It might be something or nothing. But just as I got home last night, a vintage Rolls Royce passed me. An odd-looking woman was sitting on the back seat. I... kinda got back in the car and followed it...'

'Kinda?'

'Well, I did follow it. Don't ask me why, coz I still don't know. It turned into Harrington Manor, but I daren't wait around in case she spotted me.'

'What are you saying, Sarah?'

'I asked my dad if he knew anything this morning. He said the gossip in the village was she was Finn's mother,

come to remove his personal possessions, whatever that means.'

'Well it can't be more drugs. We already know he kept his illegal activities well away from the manor. And the drugs squad searched every inch of the place.'

'All his assets are being sold by order of the state. Maybe she just wants a few things to remember him by.'

'Do you have her name?'

She heard a chuckle on the other end of the phone. 'My dad said he thought it was Cruella deVille. Given what I saw of her, that maybe wasn't so far from the truth. But Interpol said her name was Carmella deBruin, and that the Belgian police had searched her place but found nothing to implicate her.'

'I bet they didn't. If she's anything like her son, she would have covered her tracks well.'

'For sure. But it seems there was nothing to charge her with, so she's a free woman.'

'And now she's here in Norfolk. You any idea how long she's been here?'

'A few days, according to my dad. You think there's anything in that, Daisy?'

The sudden stab of dread in her stomach told Daisy part of her thought there was a lot in it. She muttered something, almost without realising she was voicing her thoughts. 'Yes, I do. It seems too much of a coincidence. I might have to pay Carmella deBruin a visit tomorrow...'

'Daisy? Please let the police handle it?'

Daisy realised she'd said words she hadn't intended saying. 'Oh Sarah, just rambling. Give me a while to think about it, please? As you say, it's likely nothing.'

'So why am I getting the feeling you don't believe that?'

'Dear, please just let me discuss it with Aidan. Keep this to yourself, just a while longer? I promise I'll get back to you in the morning, and then you can tell Burrows what you've found out.'

'I can feel that barrel at my throat again, Daisy.'

She laughed. 'I told you, that's only for the bad guys.'

'And does Carmella deBruin fall into that category?'

'I don't know yet. That's why I need to... get my head around it.'

'Are you fobbing me off?'

'Would I do such a thing?'

'Yes, you would.'

'I don't know whether to be insulted or flattered.'

'Stop changing the subject. I know what you're doing.'

'No fooling an officer of the law, huh?'

'Won't stop you trying though, will it? So no funny business, ok? I'll wait for your call in the morning.'

Daisy put the phone down, and ran a shaky hand through her silver hair. She *was* fobbing Sarah off, but she'd been honest about the reason why. She did need a little time to get her head around the news.

The fact Finn's mother was in Norfolk had disturbed her. Maybe the reason was a genuine one, that she simply wanted some of her son's things so the state didn't take everything. He was going away for a very long time, after all.

But the uneasy feeling in her gut was telling her there was more to it. The rich and powerful had a tendency to retaliate when one of their own was brought down. And sadly for Daisy, she'd been there at the final showdown, and made sure Finn knew exactly who it was who'd been responsible for his fall from grace.

A doting mother would have been to see her son in prison, and been told who it was who'd ruined his life. Both of them clearly fell into the *rich and powerful* category, and she'd been in Norfolk for a few days now.

But there was another element in the mix, one that resonated with Daisy. She knew from bitter experience how it had made her feel when Celia was taken. She'd sworn to take revenge on whoever it was responsible for bringing her child so much grief.

And the dread that wouldn't leave her soul was telling her it might just be Carmella deBruin was feeling exactly the same way.

If that was the case, it would for sure be extremely bad for her health.

Chapter 20

'Oh dear Lord... not the dotty dowager again.'

It wasn't a question. Aidan already knew Daisy was on a mission once more. One look at the pink sweat-pants and the tweed attire as she walked into the kitchen was enough to set the butterflies boxing again.

'This really isn't a good idea, dear,' he said, knowing it was a terrible idea, but that there wasn't a damn thing he could do about it.

She sipped the morning coffee he'd made for her. 'I know it's not ideal Dip, but I need to find out if she had anything to do with my murder.'

'So what are you going to do... ask her point blank?'

She kissed him softly. 'Of course not. But if she'll sit down and talk to a friendly resident of the village, I'll be able to suss her out. Then I'll know if the threat is coming from her, or if we're back to square one again.'

'And then we'll involve the police, yes?'

'Of course, dear.'

He shook his head, pulled on his shoes. 'Sometimes I wish you wouldn't pretend to agree with me so much, dear.'

Daisy ignored that, concentrated instead on getting into her boots and tweed jacket. 'I want you to drop me a little way short of the manor, and then disappear. I'll walk the rest, and then call you when I'm done. Is that okay, dear?'

'Not really. I should come with you,' he huffed.

'Dip, the last time I visited the manor you spent time with the staff, remember? They're bound to still be there, and you will be recognised.'

'And you won't?'

She flicked her dark brown locks. 'Hopefully not in this wig!'

'I still think it's too dangerous. Walking into a potential spider's web.'

'Dear, even if she susses me out, she's hardly going to try anything in her son's manor house, is she? And anyway, from what Sarah says it not a spider's web... more of a dog house!'

He groaned out his frustration, and didn't raise a smile over her joke that attempted to lighten the mood. She was already heading to the car, so he grabbed the keys and followed her out, still knowing there wasn't a damn thing he could do about it.

He pulled to a stop a quarter-mile from the entrance to the manor. 'I'll go see Sarah's father while you're in the dog house. So I'm close by, in case you get bitten.'

She smiled, glad Aidan was entering into the spirit, if extremely reluctantly. 'Thank you, dear. Just... just please don't tell him where I am. Best not to worry too many people right now.'

'Fair enough. I'll just do all the worrying instead.'

'Oh, come on, Dip. I'll be totally fine. I'm just having a friendly chat with the new lady of the manor.'

She climbed out of the car, trying to ignore the pained expression on his face. It wasn't doing her spirit any good to see he was just as worried as she was. 'Say hello to David for me, dear,' she called back as she walked away and waved to him.

The car drove off, and suddenly Daisy felt very alone. She couldn't stop her eyes looking ahead to the brick pillars of the entrance to the manor, set into the long walls that stretched fifty yards either side. Somehow it was starting to look like the gates of hell.

She shook away the image as she began to walk. All she was doing was having a nice chat with the new village resident, after all.

The new village resident who wanted her dead.

She shook that thought away too. Other than coincidence and the ache of dread in her stomach, there were no actual facts to say that Finn's mother was responsible for the attempt on her life. It could all be the ramblings of an imaginative, senile mind. Or the sheer desperation of needing to find someone to blame.

But as she made the gateway, and heard her feet crunch on the compacted gravel of the forecourt as they made their way on autopilot past the vintage Rolls towards the old oak doors, she couldn't help but feel that, spider's web or dog house, she was walking right into it.

She reached out a hand that was only slightly shaky, and pulled the brass rod of the ancient doorbell. She heard the old-fashioned tuneful ring of real brass doorbells, and then the patter of small feet as someone reached the door and pulled back a graty old latch.

Then one of the doors was pulled open, and the face of a middle-aged woman smiled a nervous greeting. 'Yes, can I help you?'

'*Hello,*' Daisy boomed. 'I'm so glad to meet you. I'm Flora Bundy, chair of the parish council. I've just called to say hello, and welcome the new resident of the village.'

'Oh... I'm not... um, Madam. I'm Mrs. Thompson, the housekeeper. I'm afraid Madam doesn't take visitors.'

Daisy already knew the woman wasn't the one she'd come to see. She was a mile from Sarah's description. 'Oh, nonsense. I'm sure she'll be happy to know how friendly we all are here.' She invited herself in, pushed past the housekeeper who'd clearly had instructions to call the lady of the house 'Madam', and even more implicit instructions to not let anyone in. 'Just tell Mrs. deBruin I'm here to see her, please.'

Mrs. Thompson looked like a frightened mouse trapped between two hungry cats, but nodded and scurried off through a door. Daisy looked around the large main hall, grunted disparagingly at the wide grand staircase that rose from the centre of the room and then split off in both directions into galleried landings giving access to the first floor bedrooms, and another staircase to the second-floor ones.

Cardboard boxes and old-style Edwardian trunks stood in various piles on the flagstone floor of the hall. Daisy grunted again; it looked like the lady of the house actually was packing up Finn's belongings for him after all. She wondered just how much stuff was already packed that the police might be interested in.

She didn't have too long to spend wondering. Mrs. Thompson was back, the nervous smile still on her face, even though it didn't seem she felt at all like smiling. 'Madam will see you now,' she muttered, in the kind of way that missed out a few words. Like *'if she has to.'*

'Good. Lead the way, my dear.'

The woman led her through a doorway into a large inner hall dotted with big potted plants and a multitude of doorways. Then she stopped, outside a mahogany door with a brass handle that Daisy knew well.

'Madam is in the library,' Mrs. Thompson said as she opened the door.

Daisy swallowed hard. She'd been into that room before, the one Finn called his office. It was the room where she'd sown the seeds of the sting that eventually led to his downfall.

Now she was about to sow a different kind of seed, one that might flourish very quickly into the bush that revealed its true colours.

She smiled confidently to the housekeeper, and strode into the room, wishing the confidence she was trying to exude was as real she was desperately telling herself it was.

Chapter 21

The sight that greeted her was a little strange, to say the least.

Daisy was vaguely aware of the housekeeper closing the door, shutting her into the dungeon of the dog house with a dull clunk. But the vision in black and white that looked her over in a disdainful fashion kind of took all her attention.

She was sitting in a large, chintz Louis-the-fifteenth armchair, an old leather-bound book on her lap she was apparently reading. Whatever it was, it was likely a first edition, pulled from the floor-to-ceiling bookcases that lined three walls. Between her fingers, a cigarette in a slim, Edwardian holder, sent gentle wisps of smoke into the aristocratic air.

Her mid-length bob of black hair was broken up by thick streaks of tinted white. She wore a long white gown, every edge trimmed with a wide black textured silk; the collar, each front panel, and the hem. A silver chair hung around her slim neck, ending with some kind of black gemstone. Beneath the open gown, a black and white Mary Quant-style dress was short enough to reveal slender, perfectly-shaped legs, draped in sheer black stockings.

Despite the fact she was apparently relaxing at home, her feet were clad in dark red stilettos, the only bit of colour to be seen anywhere on her apart from bright red lipstick. On the floor either side of the chair, two dogs sat obediently, looking like Cleopatra's sphinxes.

They were Dalmatians. And Carmella deBruin looked about forty-five years old.

Daisy threw her a false smile. She'd taken an instant dislike to her, even leaving aside she might be the woman trying to kill her. 'Oh, I'm sorry. I was expecting to meet Mr. Finnegan's mother, not his sister.'

The woman shook her head, like a matron at a boarding school. She spoke in clipped, Belgian tones, reminding Daisy of a female version of Hercule Poirot. 'I *am* his mother. My housekeeper tells me you are... Flora Bundy, from the parish council?'

Daisy widened the smile, even though it was the last thing she felt like doing. 'One and the same. Gosh, you look so... young. How do you do it? Any tips would be appreciated.'

Carmella deBruin was still shaking her head. 'Forgive me, but I doubt you could afford the, um... expert help I receive.'

'Oh, I see. So you've had a tuck or two?'

'Are you here to welcome me to the village, or insult me?'

'I'm sorry. May I sit? My poor old feet don't like standing up for too long.'

'Perhaps you should lose a little weight?' She nodded curtly to the matching chintz sofa, and took a long draw on the cigarette holder. Daisy trotted over to the sofa, noticing that unfortunately the Persian rug seemed to be devoid of muddy wellington boot prints from her last visit. Isobella the maid must have spent a few hours removing all traces of them.

She sat slowly on the sofa, like she was in awe of her surroundings, and the strange woman who appeared to belong in a bygone era. 'Nice dogs. May I ask, where are the other ninety-nine?'

'I'm sorry?'

'Never mind. Just my silly sense of humour. So... what brings you to East Winch, my dear?'

102

She let out an elegant sigh, like she really didn't want to be bothered by fake welcoming conversation. 'I am sure you are aware, Mrs. Bundy, that my son has been falsely accused of crimes he had no part in?'

'*Falsely* accused?'

'Indeed.' She paused for dramatic effect, just like Poirot, and sucked in another draw of cigarette smoke. 'I will presume you, like most others in this pitiful little village, believe my son is guilty?'

'But... the word is he was caught with the drugs in his possession?'

For a moment she looked uncomfortable. 'It will be shown that his butler, Johnson, was the one responsible. Not that it's any of your business, but he was carrying out his disgraceful operation right under my son's nose. It is positively shocking.'

'Oh, I agree. So is Mr. Finnegan going to get off then?'

'Of course. He is totally innocent.'

'But I noticed you are packing up his personal possessions, and the manor is up for sale. Doesn't that rather contradict the fact he's totally innocent?'

Carmella looked even more uncomfortable. 'It is just a precaution, in case your pathetic justice system does not listen to reason.'

'Oh, I see.'

She fixed black eyes made even blacker by thick mascara into her visitor. 'I see from your tone you would rather believe the media than me?'

'Well... you see, Carmella. Can I call you Carmella? You see, Carmella... there was an ex-copper who lives here in the village, a friend of mine, and he was apparently at Morston Quay when Mr. Finnegan was apprehended. From

103

what he tells me, it was pretty much a... slam dunk, is that what they say?'

Her tone changed. She spoke slower, and huskier. 'Are you telling me he was instrumental in bringing my son down?'

Daisy swallowed hard. The suddenly-present new version of the Belgian aristocrat was a little scarier, but she'd also realised by leading the conversation the way she had, she might have put Sarah's father in danger. She had to pull him out of it again. 'Oh no dear... he was just an observer. Didn't have any part of it. But I hear someone did? An old woman, who got her teeth into your son?'

The woman in white and black sucked a huge lungful of smoke from the cigarette. The words were growled out, even though she tried to disguise the emotion. 'I see you know a lot about this matter, Mrs. Bundy.'

'Flora dear, please.'

'Yes, there was a woman involved. A nosy bitch who wouldn't stop harassing him. Then she got entirely the wrong idea, and... well, you know the rest.'

'Hmm... I can't be doing with nosy bitches either, Carmella.'

She pulled herself together, likely realising she was saying too much to the already-converted. 'No, Flora. Neither can I. But her nosy interfering will come back to bite her.'

'Really, dear? How so?'

'Tea?' Carmella picked up an elaborately-shaped bone china teapot from the tray sitting on the walnut occasional table standing just in front of her, poured brown liquid into two equally-elaborate cups sitting on saucers. She passed one to Daisy.

'How kind.'

Carmela took a tiny sip from her cup. 'My son is a good boy. He travels to Belgium to see me very often.'

'Yes, I heard. Not that he'll be doing that for a while. So... are you here to stay?'

'Heavens, no. Quite honestly I cannot see the attraction of this exceedingly boring part of the world. I shall be returning home in a few days.'

'Oh, I'm sorry. A few days? Then we won't get the chance to become friends.'

'No, we won't, will we.'

Daisy took another sip of her tea. 'I must say, this tea is *soo* nice, Carmella.'

'Of course. It is Belgian. Would you like a slice of cake to go with it? My butler Henri, he makes the most delicious cakes. You must try some.'

'Well...'

Carmella didn't wait for an answer. She picked up the receiver of an old-fashioned brass phone by her side. 'Henri, please bring one of your delectable cakes. Our guest would like a slice.'

She threw a big beaming, terribly false smile to her guest. 'He will be here in a minute. Top up?'

Daisy handed the cup and saucer back to her. Then behind her, she heard the door open. A few seconds later, Henri came into her view, carrying a huge cake on a silver tray. He bent over, placed the tray on the occasional table. And Daisy felt the thump of dread thunder right into her soul.

Henri was tall, gangly, and dressed in the kind of formal butler-type attire that butlers used to wear in the distant past.

And he was just about as black-skinned as an African could possibly get.

105

Chapter 22

He didn't look at Daisy straight away. Something she was extremely grateful for. She tried to pull herself together, hope neither he nor the lady of the manor had noticed her shock. She tried to take her mind off the person who had baked it by focussing on the cake instead.

It was a good six inches tall, round, and covered from base to tip in dark chocolate. Across the top was a myriad of white chocolate buttons, polka-dot fashion.

It was the perfect cake for the black and white lady of the manor.

Finally Henri's dark eyes flicked to Daisy. There was no recognition in them, but then again she was wearing a wig, and he'd likely had instructions to simply rig the bomb. If he had actually set eyes on her, it could only have been from a distance.

She breathed a sigh of relief. Henri was smiling. 'May I cut you a slice, madam?'

Daisy nodded meekly. Carmella was smiling too, genuinely this time. 'Henri is my butler and... personal assistant. He is so multi-talented.'

'I bet he is.'

'Sorry?'

'I said I'm sure he is. The cake looks wonderful.'

Henri had a knife in his hand. He reached out to the cake, began to cut into it. As he did so the sleeve of his jacket rode up, and as she watched in silent fear, Daisy noticed something.

'Oh, Henri... there's a big plaster on the back of your hand. Have you had an accident?'

'Oh, it is nothing, madam. An altercation with a kitchen knife, that is all.'

'Oh, you poor thing. You must be a devil with a knife!'

He looked at her slightly curiously. Then he cast his eyes back to the cake, handed her the slice on a bone-china plate. 'Please, enjoy.'

'Oh, I will. Thank you.'

He nodded, and straightened up. 'Will there be anything else, Madam?'

Carmella smiled to him, in a certain kind of way. 'For now, no thank you, Henri. A little later you can turn down my bed, when I am ready for my afternoon nap.'

He nodded again, and left the room. Daisy matched her host's smile. 'He must be invaluable to you, Carmella. Such a polite *young* man.'

'Oh he is. I don't know what I would do without him.'

Daisy bit her lip. She would have loved to say that there were plenty of products available in discreet packaging that might help, but she decided it wasn't really the proper thing to say. Instead she asked a slightly more innocent question. 'Are you not having any chocolate cake, Carmella?'

'Good grief no. I can't abide the stuff.'

'What, cake?'

'No, chocolate. My husband was big in chocolate, you know.'

'I had a Santa Claus like that once. Until I bit his head off anyway.'

'My husband died six years ago.'

'Oh. Sorry. But you made your fortune in chocolate...'

'Belgian chocolate.'

'In Belgian chocolate, but you can't stand the stuff?'

'Flora, when your husband comes home every night for thirty years smelling of the stuff, one tends to get a bit of an aversion to it.'

'Yes, I can imagine. But it made you rich.'

'Oh yes. I sold the business after his death, for rather a lot of money.'

Daisy picked up the cake fork her murderer had given her, began to cut off a piece of the cake. 'I assume you reverted to your maiden name after he passed?'

'Yes. Finnegan didn't have quite the same ring to it as deBruin, not in the circles I move in, anyway.'

'I'm sure.'

She saw her host glance up, her artificially-enhanced hearing picking up a noise somewhere the other end of the house. Then Daisy heard it too, the banging of doors, the sound of voices.

Carmella didn't look too pleased. 'Oh, for goodness sake. The servants my son employed, they do not know what respect is.'

'You just can't get the staff these days.' Daisy shook her head, speared the first piece of cake with the fork. She was just lifting it to her mouth when the voices got suddenly louder.

She glanced around, the cake fork level with her mouth. The library door burst open, and three people ran into the room, in a hell of a hurry. One of them cried out.

'Stop!'

Chapter 23

'Don't eat that cake!'

Officer Sarah Lowry strode into the room, whipped the fork out of the hand of a stunned Daisy, and grabbed the offending cake off the occasional table and handed it to one of the officers with her.

'I was about to enjoy that!' gasped Daisy.

'Oh really, this is preposterous,' said an equally shocked Carmella deBruin.

'Take this to the lab,' said a determined Sarah. 'Analyse it for poison.'

'S... Officer, are you suggesting...' muttered Daisy.

'We have reason to believe the cake contains poison.'

'You cannot be serious. This is an infringement on my right to privacy,' Carmella spat out, finally standing up and looking like she wasn't in control any more.

'Are you serious?' said Daisy, throwing a glare into Sarah's eyes.

'Deadly serious... ok, sorry, perhaps the wrong phrase.'

'Yes, quite probably,' Daisy muttered under her breath.

Sarah wasn't to be swayed. 'Carmella deBruin, I must ask you to accompany us to the station, where you will be questioned regarding attempted poison by cake. You do not have to say anything, but anything you do say will be taken down and may be used in evidence against you.'

The lady of the manor glared at her visitor as the other female officer led her away. 'I told you the British police were *pathetic...'*

The male officer, who had placed the cake in a large evidence bad, followed them out. Sarah slipped an arm into Daisy's. 'Come along... Mrs. Bundy. I'll take you home.'

She marched a shocked-into-silence Daisy to her police car, made sure she sat in the passenger seat safely, and then dropped into the driver's seat.

Daisy wasn't prepared to be silent anymore. '*What the hell, Sarah?* Do you realise you've blown everything?'

'What... prevented you losing your life, you mean?'

'You total moron... we were getting along famously.'

'I'm not a total moron, Daisy. What were you thinking of, walking blindly into the spider's web like that?'

'I wasn't blind. And it was more of a dog house...'

'Stop being flippant. This was one idiotic step too far, Daisy.'

'Did you really think that cake was poisoned? A cake that must have been baked before my unannounced visit?'

'Well... no, maybe I didn't. I just had to get you out of there.'

Daisy threw frustrated hands into the air. 'And now you've pissed the lady of the manor off, and she's likely to react to that. And it was all going so well...'

'Quite honestly, I don't care if I pissed her off or not. I just care... care about your safety.'

As they left the manor and took the road to Great Wiltingham, Daisy melted, like a soft ice cream on the hottest day of the year. '*Oh Sarah*... I know you care. But now an unofficial line of enquiry is blown, and Carmella knows the police are on to her.'

'That's just tough. Daisy, I'm sorry, but I had to get you out of there.'

'Why? How did you even know I was there this morning anyway?'

'Um... Aidan told me.'

'I'll kill him.'

110

'He didn't mean to. I called you because you said you'd call me and you didn't. Your phone was off, so I called the house phone. He said you were out, and it didn't make sense your phone was off, so I asked him where you were... kind of forcefully. He told me then, likely because I gave him no choice.'

'I see.'

'Then he said he was worried about what you were doing, so I got worried too. And me being me, I had to do something about it.'

'Like arresting the lady of the manor on a trumped-up charge.'

'It might not have been trumped-up.'

'Adde is there.'

'What?'

'Adde is there, but he's called Henri now, apparently. He's m'lady's personal assistant, whatever that entails. Probably not difficult to imagine, if you have a mind like mine.'

'*Oh my god...* so I actually did the right thing, getting you out of there.'

'Sarah dear... do you really think they're going to do away with me in the manor? Seriously?'

'Ok... perhaps not.'

'Definitely not.'

'Well you might be happy to be the worm on the hook, but no one else is.'

'I wouldn't exactly say *happy*, Sarah.'

She reached out a hand, squeezed Daisy's. 'I'm sorry, Daisy. I care about you, very much. Even if you are a crazy old biddie.'

'Yeah, can't argue with that. But this crazy old biddie has managed to find the link. The delectable, oddball Carmella deBruin wants me dead for wrecking her son's life, and she's got the perfect personal assistant to do it for her.'

The car pulled into Daisy's drive. 'Yeah, we know who is responsible now. But the evidence he planted the bomb is circumstantial. CPS would throw it out and laugh. He got scratched by Maisie's cat, and there's evidence to prove that, but from the prosecution's point of view, that could have happened while he was walking by one night.'

'No fingerprints or tell-tale evidence from forensics then?'

'Not a jot. He knew exactly what he was doing in covering his tracks.'

'Hmm... thank you for the lift home. I need to go talk with Aidan now.'

'Don't be too hard on him, please?'

'Oh I won't. Just go and make peace with the lady of the manor, pretty please?'

'Now you're asking the impossible again.'

'What in hell's name were you thinking, Dip?'

'Nice to see you too, dear.' He glanced up from the newspaper he was pretending to read. Daisy was standing over him, spitting fire. Literally, it kind of felt like.

'Why did you turn your phone off?' he spat back.

'I... didn't want to be disturbed.' The flames subsided, the look on his face extinguishing them in seconds. *'Oh, Aidan dear...'*

He stood up, just in time to almost be bowled back to the armchair as Daisy threw herself at him, and held on like he was a lifebelt in a stormy sea. *'You and Sarah are a pain in my butt, you know that?'* she whispered into his shoulder.

He was about to tell her she was exactly the same, but then felt the shakes of her body against his, and heard the

112

sob she tried to suppress. He held her tight against him until he felt her relax, and then eased her away and dried her tears with a handkerchief.

'I suppose I could have said you'd gone to see Maisie, but Sarah wasn't taking prisoners. She'd tried to call you, and realised you'd never turn your phone off just to visit a friend in the village.'

'Guess I should have left it on.'

She told him of her morning, and as he brewed coffee and listened to every word, he let out a mirthless chuckle at Sarah's trumped-up reason for intervening.

'She has your spirit dear, I'll say that much.'

'That's what worries me.'

Chapter 24

Aidan decided to cook a roast to take his mind off depressing thoughts, and grabbed a leg of lamb from the freezer. While Daisy made a redcurrant sauce, they discussed the possible repercussions of Sarah's well-meaning but possibly damaging intervention.

'The delectable Carmella will be well annoyed with life now.'

'Yes, she will. Positively fuming. And that might make a difference to everyone's life now.'

Daisy screwed up her face. 'Or death. She could go two ways; either give up and go back to Belgium to lick her wounds, or be even more determined to exact her revenge before she does go back.'

Aidan arranged some roast potatoes and parsnips in a baking tray, shoved it into the oven. 'Either way, Sarah's antics have forced her hand. Whatever she decides to do, she knows there isn't much time left.'

'She said she was going home in a few days anyway.'

'We might need to be on our guard, Flower.'

A waft of dull ache drifted through Daisy's stomach. 'At least we know who it is trying to end my life now. Perhaps we should take it in turns to sleep tonight?'

He pulled her into a hug, seeing the dull ache even though it wouldn't have been obvious to anyone else. 'I think that might be a good idea,' he said quietly.

Daisy picked up her phone. 'I'll text Sarah, see if she fancies roast lamb. Then she can tell us how the interrogation went.'

A rather quiet and sheepish Sarah walked through the kitchen door. Daisy gave her a hug and a beaming smile, just so she knew there was no lasting animosity.

'So how's the lady of the manor?'

'Pissed off. Threatening to sue the arse off Norfolk police.'

'No big surprise there. She won't though... in the circumstances she's wise enough to know she'll have to swallow the pill and smile sweetly.'

'I've made things worse, haven't I?'

Daisy pulled out a chair at the table, beckoned her to sit. 'No dear... but you've very likely accelerated them. How's your grumpy boss?'

'Grumpy. He's told me if she sues he'll have my badge.'

Daisy put a hand on her arm. 'Your badge is safe, Sarah.'

'Anyway, what do you mean, accelerated things?'

'Aidan and I were discussing it earlier. Now Carmella knows the police are on to her, she'll either bugger off home with her tail between her legs, or bring killing me forward, while she still can.'

'There's nothing like telling it like it is, is there Daisy?'

Daisy chuckled, but there wasn't a lot of mirth in it. 'No point in beating around the bush, dear. We now know who wants me gone, and that in her mind there's a very good reason why. It all depends how far she's prepared to go, given the fact she was just arrested on related charges.'

'So you're saying my inept police work might have fired her up to be even more determined to do the deed?'

'Quite possibly, yes.'

Aidan served up the roast, and saw the unhappy look on their guest's face. He took his seat, tried to smile encouragingly. 'On the other hand, now she knows the police are interested, she might just forget all about it. So you might have done us a favour, even though your motives weren't police-related at all.'

'I still used my career and my uniform to get Daisy out of a dangerous situation though. Burrows wants a full report, including how I knew the cake might be poisoned... and I don't know what the hell to say to exonerate myself.'

Daisy felt a pang of harsh memory, put down her fork and gave Sarah a hug. The sad look on her face, and the tone of her words, had reminded her of something she didn't want to remember.

When Celia first got hooked on drugs... as they found out later, deliberately groomed by Briggs as a prelude to being taken... the sad, desperate look and tone in her voice was exactly the same as Sarah's.

The déjà vu, and the unhappiness of her friend, was almost too much to take. Daisy had hugged Sarah just as much for herself as she had for her friend.

'Look Sarah, you did what you thought was right, and that's all that really matters. A certain peculiar Belgian woman and a DCI might not see it that way, but we do. Before you go we'll scribble out a draft report for you to write for Burrows tomorrow, so he doesn't know you've been keeping things from him. Deal?'

She finally smiled. 'Deal. Thank you, Daisy.'

She grinned. 'It's the least we can do, I think. I take it the cake was kosher?'

Sarah nodded. 'Of course. The guys in the lab said it was delicious.'

'At least it didn't go to waste,' Aidan grinned.

Daisy's eyes narrowed. 'I've just had a thought.'

Aidan looked up from his plate, a pained expression on his face. 'Oh dear.'

'Now don't be like that, dear. You know my thoughts are usually... well, sensible. Sometimes.'

'If you say so, dear.'

'Well, I was thinking... if nothing happens tonight, I think I might pop round to the manor tomorrow, show the dear lady a bit of sympathy from the parish council.'

'What?' cried Aidan.

'Seriously? I just got you out of the dog house, and now you want to run right back in?' said Sarah, shaking her head like she couldn't believe what she was hearing.

'Hear me out. When you bungled in... sorry, Sarah... I was just working up to finding out more about Adde. Well, Henri, apparently. There's a possibility the lady of the manor doesn't know about his shady past. A past that...' she pierced a stare into Aidan. 'Might have involved abducting our daughter, dear. According to Roland Spence, he was once an associate of Briggs. Has it occurred to you he might know something about Celia being trafficked?'

He sat back, lifted his eyes to the ceiling. 'It has now.'

'So do you both see where this is going? Somehow I need to be close to that piece of filth, force his hand. Maybe win back Carmella's trust, find out if he's pulled the wool, or the Dalmatian hair, over her eyes. Perhaps if she knows just how much of a criminal he actually is, she might decide he's too much of a risk to have around. Even as her...um, personal assistant.'

'That's a few sentences-worth of long shots, dear.'

'Yes I know, Dip. But the only way to find out how much of a long shot they are is to go make peace with the lady of the manor. So tomorrow I'm going to visit again, just for a chat. A chat she won't realise is going to answer a few more questions.'

117

'You're insane. But I can see the logic,' said Aidan as he shook his head despairingly.

'So can I,' said Sarah. 'But you're not damn well going alone. I'm coming with you.'

'Sarah...'

'No arguments. If you say no I'll just arrest you on another trumped-up charge.'

'You actually mean that, don't you?'

'You'd better believe it.'

Aidan was nodding his head. 'Actually dear, it does make logical sense if you think about it. The chair of the parish council and a representative of Norfolk police, calling round to apologise for the misunderstanding, and then grovelling like hell. She'd love that.'

'You mean I've got to grovel to her?' Daisy growled.

'Just pretend, dear.'

'If I have to.'

'Oh, just one thing though,' Sarah said. It's Burrows day off tomorrow, and I'll have to be working all day. But we can go in the evening. Pick you up at seven, deal?'

Daisy shook her head, but she knew she had little choice but to agree, with everyone ganging up on her. 'Deal.'

Chapter 25

Daisy and Aidan took it in turns to keep watch that night, each doing three-hour shifts. Other than Brutus, who came seeking his saucer of semi-skimmed, no one else appeared.

As the light of morning sent autumn sunbeams across the garden, they both breathed a sigh of relief. Neither had got a full night's sleep, but the daylight had brought a sense of comfort, and a sense of frustration for Daisy.

She'd been ready for her Nigerian murderer; ready to defend herself in any way it took, but clearly *he* wasn't ready to carry on where he'd left off. It was almost a disappointment, because if he'd forced endgame, she'd been quite prepared to bring about *his* endgame, if it has proved necessary.

Now she was left with a day of trying to find things to do to keep busy, and an evening visit to the lady of the manor to do the last thing she felt like doing... grovelling a fake apology to the one person who really didn't deserve it.

She and Aidan spent the day doing housework that seriously didn't need doing, and late in the afternoon Daisy found herself in the bedroom she'd set aside for Celia, even though most of her had believed their daughter would never use it. She picked up the photo of the three of them, taken when Celia was fifteen, and sat on the bed, running a gentle, loving finger across it in an absent-minded kind of way.

The visit to Roland Spence had given her a vague kind of unexpected hope. From what he'd said, their daughter wasn't dead. But it was hardly much consolation, knowing she could be virtually anywhere in the world, trafficked to a rich and powerful man who wasn't exactly likely to admit he'd bought her.

Even if they could find out who he was, and where he lived. Which was next to impossible, when the whole world was a possibility.

But a seed of hope had suddenly begun to shoot up from nowhere. The man who was trying to murder her was also the one who might know where Celia was. Two days ago she'd discovered the thug who shopped Spence ran a secret two-way trafficking operation, and one of the people he associated with was Adde Wambua.

It was the tiniest seed of hope. The Nigerian might have had nothing to do with the trafficking operation. And even if he did, their daughter may have been just another pretty face to him, long gone and long forgotten.

But it was still a tiny seed. And Daisy knew if it was to eventually bear fruit, Adde Wambua had to stay alive. Long enough for her to find out if he knew anything, at least.

Daisy smiled sadly, said a fond goodnight to her daughter, and carefully placed the framed photo back on the shelf above the dressing table.

In a couple of hours it would be time to grovel to Carmella deBruin, and sow her own first seeds of discovery. Whether they would bear fruit, it was impossible to know.

Sarah picked Daisy up just before seven. The last light of day was saying farewell as they drove the short distance to Harrington Manor.

'You in grovelling mode, Daisy?'

'No, but I can switch it on.' She threw Sarah a big, false smile, just so she knew she could.

'Ouch... don't overdo it, Flora.'

Daisy grinned. 'Don't worry. There's far too much dislike flying around to gush too much.'

'Not your favourite person, huh?'

'Well dear... leaving aside the fact she's a vengeful, murderous bitch who will stop at nothing to make sure no one gets in the way of her posh lifestyle... I actually can't stand the woman.'

'Ouch again... maybe that false beaming smile is the best thing after all.'

'Coming right up, my dear.'

Sarah turned the car into the entranceway, drove through the large brick pillars just as the last of the sun's rays disappeared, and draped the forecourt in almost-dark shadows that felt kind of ominous.

The Rolls was parked close to the front door. Sarah drew up alongside it, switched off the motor. Then she pierced a stare into her passenger.

'Just be nice. No funny business, ok?'

'I can't shoot her in the stilettos then?'

'You didn't bring you gun. *Did you?*'

'Of course not. I'll be nice, promise.'

'Make sure you are. The last thing we need is you upsetting her again.'

'Excuse me? If I remember right, it was you who upset her the first time.'

'Oh yes. Fair point. My bad.'

'Let's just go and get this over with.'

They walked to the doors, and Daisy pulled the brass rod again. And again, they heard the merry jingle of real bells, followed by the sound of the latch being drawn back, and Mrs. Thompson's face peering at them.

'Oh good evening, Mrs. Thompson. Sorry to disturb you at this hour, but we've come to gr... apologise to Carmella for the upsetting incident yesterday.'

'Oh... I see,' Mrs. Thompson said, a little uncertainly.

'May we please come in?'

The housekeeper stood aside, allowed her visitors to enter the hallway. The boxes and trunks were still stacked in the floor. No one else seemed to be around. 'May we see Carmella please, just for a few minutes?'

'Um... no, I'm sorry but you can't.'

Daisy glanced to Sarah. She'd expected a little reluctance, but not a downright refusal. 'Excuse me... why not?'

'I'm sorry, but you've had a wasted journey. Mrs. deBruin left this morning. She's gone back to Belgium, and she won't be coming back, thank god.'

Chapter 26

Daisy's heart sank. In one way it was a relief; with the lady of the manor back in her Belgian manor, it would seem to indicate she'd given up on retribution, at least for the time being. But on the other hand, she'd lost the opportunity to find out more that might have incriminated her in attempted murder.

And she'd lost the opportunity to discover what Adde Wambua knew about Celia's disappearance.

But then something occurred to her. 'Mrs. Thompson... the Rolls is still on the forecourt?'

She shook her head, looked like her personal hell wasn't yet over. 'That so-called chauffeur and... personal assistant of hers, Henri, he's still here. Mrs. deBruin caught a flight home. He's driving it back tomorrow, with some of these boxes.'

'Oh, I see.' Suddenly, a faint ray of hope reappeared for Daisy. Maybe all was not lost. 'So he's here? Perhaps we should apologise to him instead?'

Mrs. Thompson shook her head again. 'Would you like a cup of tea? I've just brewed up in my sitting room.'

Daisy glanced to Sarah, who nodded. 'That would be nice, thank you.'

They followed the housekeeper through a door, and into a passageway that was nowhere near as elegant as the rest of the house. It was clearly the servant's quarters, but as Mrs. Thompson opened a door and led them through, her sitting room was nicely furnished. Just not as expensively as the main house.

She poured tea into two smart mugs, handed them to her guests. 'Please, sit. I'm afraid my sofa isn't as elegant as the one you sat on before, but at least it's comfortable. And I don't do that fancy bone china stuff, so I hope a mug is acceptable.'

'Oh, neither do I, dear,' Daisy grinned, thinking to herself the sofa and the mug were plenty acceptable enough, and a damn site cosier than the aristocratic offerings of the previous day.

'When we've had our tea, we should perhaps offer our apologies to Henri though, Mrs. Thompson?'

'Call me Irene, please. But you can't see that Henri either, I'm afraid. I saw him leave a half-hour ago.'

'Leave?'

'I suppose he's popped out, to the pub or something. He took the estate Landrover. *Madam* doesn't allow him to drive that posh car unless he's driving her, or driving it somewhere to pick her up.'

'Didn't he tell you what time he'd be back?'

'You've got to be joking. He thinks he's just as posh as his *madam*.'

Daisy had to grin, in a gruesome kind of way. She tried not to let it show. 'I'm guessing by your tone there's not a lot of love lost?'

'Him? He's just a thug who got lucky. They're the worst kind, you know. They're suddenly the flavour of the month, and they can't handle the adoration. As if that freak of nature in black and white wasn't enough.'

This time Daisy chuckled out loud. 'She's a freak of nature alright... part human, part dinosaur, part Dalmatian.'

Mrs. Thompson laughed too. 'I couldn't have put it better myself. Mr. Finnegan, crook as he was, always treated us with respect. His mother treated me like she'd just scraped me off her stiletto. Good riddance to her, I say.'

Sarah shook her head in a sympathetic kind of way. 'Perhaps when the manor is sold, the new owners will treat you well, Irene?'

She lowered her head. 'When the house is sold, I'll very likely be out of a job, dear. The new owners will be rich enough to have their own staff, who will almost certainly come with them. And I'm fifty-five now, so the likelihood of me finding another position is remote, to say the least.'

A wave of sadness passed through Daisy. Irene was all too right. She likely would be out of a job, and it was ultimately Daisy's doing. Finn had to be brought down, but she was just beginning to realise the repercussions of that would affect a lot of people for a long time to come.

Including her, if she didn't do something about it.

But Irene hadn't finished with her revelations. She pierced a stare into Daisy. 'Please forgive me for saying, but you're not the chair of the parish council, are you?'

Daisy could hold the stare. It was always a possibility those who had lived locally for years would know who she wasn't, and the housekeeper sure fitted that description. 'No, I'm not, Irene. I'm someone with a much more serious agenda. And Henri isn't Henri either.'

Sarah glanced to her in horror. *'Daisy...'*

Irene's eyes opened wide. *'Daisy?* So you're not Flora at all?'

Daisy narrowed her eyes at Sarah, who mouthed a silent *'sorry'*. 'No, Irene. We're here because madam blames me for ruining her son's life, and tried to kill me.'

'Oh goodness gracious... the bomb in Great Wiltingham? It was all over the news. But... someone died, didn't they?'

'Yes. An innocent man, tragically. Which is why we're here now. The thug who is still here had something to do with it. Not that that will come as any surprise to you, Irene.'

'I knew he was trouble.'

Daisy walked over to the bureau, wrote her number on the pad sitting there. 'Truth is Irene, they're both trouble. But now I want you to do something for me, if you would. Stay in your room tonight, and when Henri gets back, you call me?'

'Shouldn't I call the police, dear?' She glanced to Sarah, still in her uniform. 'Sorry, I mean *more* police?'

'The police are already involved, Irene. This is a covert operation.'

'Oh, I say...'

'But there's no real proof yet of either of them doing anything wrong, except disrespecting this country anyway. Henri isn't going to risk hurting you, not now. But just keep out of his way tonight, and let me know when he's back.'

'Oh, I say...'

'Irene's right, you know. We should call the police.'

Daisy glanced to Sarah. They were driving back to Wiltingham through the dark lanes, and Daisy knew time was running out if she was to somehow get any useful information that would help her twin quests.

'You are the police.'

'You know what I mean.'

'Sarah, all due respect to the police and all that, but you know as well as I do Adde will clam up if you arrest him now. He's only going to squeal if there's some benefit in it for him, and admitting he was part of Celia's abduction in a trafficking ring the police knew nothing about will just implicate him further. And then I'll... I'll have nothing that will help me find Celia in a million years.'

126

Sarah reached out a hand. 'I know, Daisy. But this is getting dangerous now. I'm not happy, but I understand your conflict.'

'Then just give me tonight. If Irene calls me later, I'll decide what to do then. By the light of morning, if I haven't got anywhere, then you can involve Burrows... before he disappears out of the country. Is that a fair thing to ask?'

Sarah nodded reluctantly. Daisy could see by her face she was anything but happy, but the seed of hope for Celia was rapidly running out of soil to flourish in. She still didn't know how best to nurture it back to health, but it was all there was left.

The rest of the trip was made in silence. As they arrived at the cottage, Daisy could see the gate was closed.

'Just pull up outside, Sarah. Unless you want a coffee?'

'No, thanks all the same. I think my bed is calling. Early shift tomorrow. But if Irene calls, you call me, ok? Early start or not, I'm not letting you go off on a crusade without me. Deal?'

'That's my line.'

'Deal?'

'Deal.'

Sarah stopped the car right outside the pedestrian gate. Daisy glanced to the house. The big bay window was set quite low to the ground, and she could see right into the living room. The curtains were open, the floor-standing lights on.

It wasn't exactly bright, but she could see enough to make her heart miss a beat.

'Turn the headlights off,' she screamed.

'What?'

'Turn the headlights off. And back up slowly, so we're behind the bushes.'

Chapter 27

Sarah did as she was told. 'Daisy, what's wrong?'

'I just saw Aidan,' she muttered shakily.

'He does live there,' Sarah said, fearing there was more to come.

'Yes, but he's not usually tied to a chair with a gag round his mouth.'

'*Oh hell...*' Sarah pulled the phone from her coat pocket. Daisy put out a shaky hand and stopped her making the call.

'Don't, please.'

'*Daisy!* Aidan's in danger.'

She shook her head. 'He's not the one in danger. That murderous thug is in my living room, but Aidan's not the one he wants.'

'So you're just going to walk in... spider's web springs to mind again?'

Daisy thought quickly. 'No, I'm not going to *walk* in. But don't you see... this is my last opportunity to persuade that piece of filth to tell me what I want to know. I have to save Aidan, and take the last chance saloon.'

'And how are you going to do that? Threaten him with your wig?'

'My gun is in the office.'

'*Daisy!* I can't let you do that.'

'Sarah dear, I'm not going to shoot him. I'll just let him think I'm going to.'

She shook her head again, more violently this time. 'And how are you even going to get to your gun? The one you're not going to shoot him with?'

'I think the window to the downstairs' bathroom is open. At least it was when I left. It has a connecting door to the office where the gun cabinet is, which was a bedroom in a previous life. We can get in there, without him knowing.'

'You're insane.'

'Have you ever had a daughter taken, Sarah?' Daisy said curtly.

'You know I haven't,' she replied quietly.

'Then you have no idea how I'm feeling right now. Adde Wambua is the last link to the faint hope of finding out where she is. And this is the last opportunity to get him to spill. What would you do?'

'And Aidan?'

'If that thug wanted him dead, he'd be already gone. He's waiting for me. And there's something else you have no experience of. Aidan is Celia's father, and just as determined as me to take whatever steps he needs to discover where and how she is. No matter what the cost.'

Sarah lifted a hand to protest, but then groaned and let it flop to her lap again. 'I guess you make a good case, Daisy. So who am I to interfere in last chance saloon? I'm just a rookie cop who can't possibly know how you both feel.'

Daisy leant over, gave her a quick hug. 'I know you're not that lacking in the feelings department, Sarah. I was just making a point. Now can we go see if that window is open?'

They crept through the pedestrian gate, which was just away from the direct line of sight of the living room window. Keeping to the small front lawn so the gravel didn't crunch, they eased open the tall gate and tiptoed down the path at the side of the house.

Luckily the bathroom window opened onto the side path. Which was narrow, bordered on one side by the wall of the house, the other by the tall bushes of the south perimeter of the plot. It was little more than four feet across, and dark. Paved with concrete slabs, their feet made no sound as they headed along it and found the bathroom window.

Daisy looked at it in dismay. The previous owners had replaced all the windows but kept the traditional feel of the cottage. The four-foot square window was divided into three; a fixed pane, a fairly large opening light, and a much smaller opening light running across the top.

When she'd last used the bathroom the big opening frame was open, letting in the warm September air. But Aidan had closed it as the chill of the evening took hold. Only the top light was open, and it was small. And a little way above their heads.

Daisy narrowed her eyes. 'I think I can get partway through that, then reach down and open the big window. Let me climb on your shoulders, Sarah.'

'Seriously? I'm only a slip of a girl, according to you.'

'Are you saying I'm overweight?'

'No, but you're... heavier than me.'

'Very diplomatic. Ok then, I'll bend down so you can climb on my shoulders.'

'I'm not that much of a slip.'

'Just do it.'

Daisy crouched down. Sarah shook her head, not quite believing what she was doing, and straddled her shoulders. With a little help from hands grasped onto the window cill, Daisy managed to stand up.

'I'm still not high enough.'

'You'll have to stand on my shoulders then.' Daisy grabbed her flailing feet, pushed up hard until they were standing on her shoulders. Sarah was whispering out grunts. 'This window is tiny. I still can't reach the handle to the other one. You'll have to help me...'

Daisy reached up, grabbed Sara's butt and pushed hard.

'Do you mind not groping my butt cheeks?'

'For god's sake, I'm not gay, you moron. Why would I want to grope your scrawny butt anyway?'

'It's not scrawny... actually, it's quite perky...'

'Will you just get on with it?'

The unintentional butt-grope helped. With a final wheeze and a super-human effort from the rookie cop with her head and shoulders wedged through a tiny window, the large opening light was open.

Daisy thought she heard the kind of sound a suction cup makes when you disengage it, as she disentangled Sarah from her shoulders, and gasped in a few breaths. 'You can grope *my* butt now, if it makes you feel any better,' she grinned.

'Very funny. Now we can get in without being rubber-man.'

'Not *we*, dear. Help me in, then I want you to stay outside, keep watch. But no peeping through windows again, please?'

'Keep watch? For what?'

'Oh, I don't know. Any more intruders?'

'You're just fobbing me off again.'

'Yes... but if he sees you in that uniform he'll panic and clam up. So please do as I say and stay here.'

'I suppose you do have a point.'

'A very good one. So just keep you and your uniform out of sight, please.'

'And you, don't get trigger-happy, or I'll have to arrest you for possessing an illegal firearm.'

'But I have a licence, dear.'

'Yes, that ran out in another millennia.'

'Now you're saying I'm old as well as fat?'

'Just get in and do what you have to.'

Sarah crouched down, made a cradle with her hands so Daisy could step onto it. She lifted her up, and then felt the weight lessen as Daisy stuck a knee on the cill. Then she helped her in with a little butt-grope, just for good measure.

'Cheeky.'

Daisy clambered into the bath, took off her shoes, climbed out and tiptoed through the connecting door into the office, grateful once again she'd not got round to bricking it up. It was the second time she'd used it when there had been an intruder in the house. Maybe she should leave it as a door after all, for the next time it was needed.

She felt her body shudder a little at that thought. Hopefully there wouldn't be a next time.

She checked the rifle was loaded, even though she knew it was. The previous night when she'd kept watch she'd made sure the AK-47 was ready and by her side, just in case. But Aidan didn't really like her having it around, a reminder of darker times, so that morning she'd put it out of sight in its cabinet.

Right then she was so grateful she had, because if it had been in plain sight Adde Wambua would have soon spotted it, and taken great delight in using it to his advantage.

As it was, he had no idea it existed. But any minute, he would. He was just about to find himself firmly on the wrong side of it.

Chapter 28

Quietly, Daisy eased open the door to the inner hall. It was in darkness, luckily. She listened for any sounds of movement, but all she could hear was the faint gurgling of the coffee machine coming from the kitchen area. The insolent thug must have been making himself a coffee while he waited for his target to return.

She shook away the feeling of yet another reason to put a bullet in him, reminding herself dead men don't talk. She sucked in a deep breath, psyched herself up, and told her heart to stop pounding in her chest. The man she loved was in danger, and the man she hated needed to talk.

She had to keep control, in order for both those things to be resolved.

She let the gun hang by her side, knowing it would be safer if, when the brute saw it, it wasn't pointing right at him. Then, she saw him. And heard him too. Just for a second, his tall frame passed through her narrow line of vision, strolling from the kitchen area towards the front window where Aidan was sitting. Her thinking was right; the thug had a coffee cup in one hand. The other was wrapped around a handgun. He rasped out the words, in a heavy Nigerian accent he hadn't possessed when she last saw him in the company of his mistress.

'Where that bitch of yours? I ain't got all night here. She better show soon, or there'll be a mess on this carpet.'

It was time. It had to be, before the guy infuriated her any more, and sent composure right out of the window.

She strode into the light of the living room, stood with her legs slightly apart, the gun by her side but ready for instant action.

'Who gave you permission to drink my coffee, boy?'

To say he was shocked into a frozen statue was an understatement. Not only had the woman of his dreams suddenly appeared from nowhere, she was carrying an automatic rifle which was helping turn his dream into a nightmare. And on top of all that, she was someone he recognised.

Then he got something else to further immobilise him.

'Tell you what, *Adde*. You untie Aidan, and then I'll let you drink your coffee while we talk. Is that good for you?'

For a second or two his mouth dropped open, and then it tried to form words that didn't come. Then finally he unfroze himself, lifted his arm and pointed the gun at Daisy. She grinned mirthlessly; his five seconds of shocked immobility had given her plenty of time to raise the rifle, which was now aimed right at him.

She ratcheted back the firing cylinder, making a point. 'Is that good for you, *Adde?*'

He finally managed to form words. 'You... you the lady of the cake...'

'Shame I didn't get to taste it. Sadly, the police intervened. As if you'd poison me, hey Adde?'

'My name is Henri Bouchard,' he mumbled in a small voice, the rather insignificant but still deadly gun in his hand starting to shake as he realised the lady of the cake meant business.

Daisy sneered out the words. 'I'm sure that's what your fake passport says, *Adde Wambua*.'

'How... you can't know who I am... I mean, my name is Henri Bouchard.'

'Oh come on... quit with the pretence, Adde. We know exactly who you are.'

'We... who is we?'

'Wouldn't you like to know.'

'Geez...' The handgun lifted again, its owner beginning to realise there was plenty someone else knew, and that he was desperately short of facts. 'Don't you come any nearer, lady. Or the old man gets it.'

He flicked the weapon to Aidan's forehead, who closed his eyes and tried to mumble something through the gag. It wasn't legible, so he nodded his head violently instead. Daisy could see Adde was losing his cool, knew that could end up in a trigger pulled unintentionally. She lowered the rifle, spoke softer.

'Ok, Adde. I've lowered my gun, now please lower yours. There are police officers outside, but I promise I won't involve them... if you tell me what I want to know.'

'You ain't in no position to make demands, old woman.'

'Oh really? Let me put it like this then... if you don't give me the information I'm asking for, I'll splatter your brains all over my carpet.'

'You... you's bullshitting me.'

'I see. So senile old women living in rural villages in the UK normally carry AK-47s then?'

'I... geez... who the hell are you?'

'Wouldn't you like to know.'

'Kinda would, yeah.'

'Let's just say Adde, attempting to murder me was your worst move ever. You can tell that to your mistress too, if you ever see her again.'

'You some kind of James Bond?'

'Wrong sex, boy.'

'Sure, but...at your age?'

'Now you're really starting to piss me off.'

'Ok... ok... what you want to know?'

'Undo Aidan first, please?'

135

He bent down and undid the ropes, then ripped the gag from Aidan's mouth, still somehow keeping the gun pointed at Daisy. Aidan gasped in a few deep breaths, and then threw Adde a cynical smile.

'Well, you got what you wanted, *Henri*. The person you needed to see is right in front of you now.'

He didn't look too delighted at the prospect. 'Sure... now we's all one big happy family.'

Daisy nodded to the kitchen. 'Dear, I'm gasping for a coffee. You fancy making me one?'

He lifted himself to his feet, walked a little stiffly to the kitchen, rubbing his neck. Daisy watched him go, realised he'd been sitting tied to the chair for a while. For a moment she saw yet another reason to put a bullet in the Nigerian thug, but resisted it yet again.

Getting banged up for murder would rather defeat the object of being there in the first place. And for sure stop her acting on any information she might force out of the thoroughly unpleasant guy.

She waited a moment to make sure Aidan was safely away from immediate danger, and then fixed a glare into her visitor. 'Shall we sit, Adde? My poor old feet, you know.'

He looked terrified at that prospect. 'Nah... I prefer standing, thanks.'

'I bet you do. Fair enough. Mind if I keep standing too, then?'

'You giving me a choice?'

'Not at all.' She took a deliberate step towards him. He took a step back, waving the gun around in a vague kind of way. There wasn't a lot further he could go, he was almost up against the bay window.

'So, my murderous friend... does your mistress know who you actually are?'

136

'That ain't none of your business.'

'Oh I think it is. If she employed you for your... talents, shall we call them, then she must have known you were an evil thug.'

'Hey, that ain't called for, old woman.'

'If you don't stop calling me that, my trigger finger might respond before my sensible side does.'

'Ok... ok, you ain't old... James... Jaime?'

'You can call me Daisy.'

She ripped off the wig, mostly because it was starting to itch, shook her silver hair back into some kind of line.

Adde gasped. 'Geez... now you look like Finn described...' He shut his gob, realising it had gone a sentence too far. Daisy realised it too.

'Ah, so the delectable Carmella did order you to end my life?'

'That ain't none of your business either, old... Daisy.' He grinned inanely, showing her his oversized white teeth with a tiny gap between each one, reminding her a little of Wallace and Gromit.

She decided that wasn't enough reason to pull the trigger either, especially as the inane smile was accompanied by a heavy dose of nervous uncertainty.

And she'd achieved the first objective after all.

'So your mistress did order you to kill me.'

'I told you, that ain't...'

'Just stop with the false bravado, hey Adde? We both know that leg you're standing on is crumbling to dust.'

Aidan handed her a mug of coffee. 'Listen, dear boy,' he said as Daisy took a sip. 'The harsh facts of life are that you're a dismal failure. Last time you tried you got the wrong person, and this time you've got an automatic rifle pointed at your head. And I can't guarantee my wife won't...

um, accidentally pull the trigger. Quite frankly old chap, it's not looking too good, is it?'

The pistol in his hand shook a little more. The whites of his eyes flicked around the room, like he was hoping for an escape hatch to magically appear in the floor. There was no escape, magic hatch or otherwise. He was cornered in the part of the room that had no doors, and Aidan, Daisy and a primed automatic rifle were in the way of any possible escape route.

Yet still he was going to hiss his threats like a cornered gazelle. 'Hey, I still got me a gun, see? And I ain't afraid to use it.'

Daisy handed the mug back to Aidan, tightened both hands around her gun. 'Funny that... I have a gun too. And it's bigger than yours. So how about we compromise?'

'You thinkin' I's gonna cave, lady?'

'Well, maybe. If you fire that pea-shooter those police outside will be in here in seconds, and that's the end of your freedom, Adde. And given your rather thick file, I doubt you'll be personally assisting anyone for a very long time. On the other hand...'

He took a nervous step even closer to the window. Daisy matched him with a much more assured one. 'On the other hand... you could give yourself up before you make everything worse, get a shorter sentence by implicating the lady of the manor, and I'll use my Jaime Bond influence to make sure you get the best deal possible. I hear you're quite good at squealing.'

'Sure... like you'd do that for the likes of me.'

Aidan interceded. 'Actually, my wife will. And I'll back her up. But only if you tell us something else we really need to know. Something that is even more important to us than implicating Carmella.'

His coal-black brow furrowed into a frown. 'I ain't got nothin' you want that's worth nothin'.'

'Oh but you have... well, maybe. Shall we find out how valuable you are?'

Daisy lifted the gun higher on her shoulder, gave him as menacing a stare as she could manage. But it was hiding a thumping, racing heart. The moment had come, and suddenly the enormity was almost too much to bear. The feeling in her gut that Adde Wambua knew something about Celia's abduction was either going to be confirmed, or shattered into tiny pieces.

The thug might not have a leg to stand on any more, but on that one at least, he held all the cards.

Chapter 29

'So, Adde. What's inside your head is your bargaining tool. Tell us where our daughter is, and you've got a deal.'

'Your... *daughter?* How the hell am I supposed to know where your daughter is? She run away or something?'

His face fell, the possibility of a saving grace receding in his mind. He looked totally confused, and somewhat dejected. Daisy glanced to Aidan, a frown of vague disappointment on her brow. The thug who could suddenly looked like the thug who can't, and his confusion was genuine. He wasn't making a connection.

It crossed Aidan's mind he might need a little jolt in the right direction. 'We've been told you were part of an illegal immigration ring. Ring any bells?'

'Aw, geez... that was years ago. I ain't into that shit anymore.'

Daisy laughed cynically. 'Too busy baking cakes for dotty aristocrats, Adde?'

'Yeah, if you like.'

'We know the ring was disbanded a while back. And your mate Jason was more than involved.'

He shook his head. 'Briggs? He died in prison. Good riddance of you ask me. He was nothin' but a thug.'

Daisy raised her eyes to the ceiling. 'Oh that's rich, coming from a murderous piece of crap like you.'

'Hey, lady... um, Daisy. I got principles.'

'Yeah, the principle that if you squeal loud enough you get a lesser sentence.'

'That might be one of them, yeah.'

'You're a pathetic wimp, Adde.'

'Yeah well, talking of self-preservation societies, you promised me.'

'I promised nothing, dear boy.'

'What? Now who's wimping out?'

Aidan held up a hand. 'Daisy is right, she didn't promise you anything. But she is the one holding the gun, remember? And I said we'll deal, so just cut the crap.'

'Hey man, seems I ain't got nothin' to deal with. I ain't got a clue where your daughter is.'

'Then let me give you a kick-ass prompt. Think back three years ago.'

'Three years?'

'If I'm guessing right, our daughter was the last English girl you took, just about the time your mate Briggs was arrested and you shut everything down.'

'Geez...' The words faded away, as vague memories started to kick in.

Daisy hissed out the final prompt, noticing the recall clouding his eyes. 'Our daughter was twenty-two, petite, pretty with natural blonde hair. *Now* do you remember?'

'Hell dudes... we operated in London, not the back of beyond like here.'

'Yes, we know. At that time we lived in London, Notting Hill.'

'Oh shit.'

Now the recall was thumping into him, in the kind of relentless way that made it seem like yesterday. Daisy was all too aware how that felt, and more and more convinced he was the key she needed to unlock a three-year mystery. She tightened the gun to her shoulder, and volunteered the final piece of information he needed to complete the circuit.

'Her name was Celia Henderson.'

For a few seconds his expression didn't change. Then he began to smile an evil but uncertain smile. '*That* junkie? The dope-head who didn't know what year it was half the time? *She was your daughter?*'

Daisy felt her whole body tense, her finger close inadvertently around the trigger. The smiling thug's words were true enough, but misguided. It didn't stop old wounds being opened, and Adde Wambua was the one opening them. It was all getting a little harder to handle than she'd thought.

She noticed Aidan's fists clench, but as always he kept control. Nevertheless, the words were growled out.

'She wouldn't have been a junkie if it wasn't for that mate of yours, Briggs. He got her into it.'

Adde was treading on thin ground, but he didn't seem to realise it. '*Seriously?* From what I heard she was well past the point of no return by the time he got his teeth into her.'

Daisy could see nothing but a red mist. '*Take that back.* You have no idea.'

Adde Wambua's grin got wider. He still didn't have a leg to stand on, but he was suddenly enjoying watching two doting parents squirming with harsh facts he was in control of dishing out, even if they weren't entirely truthful.

Daisy hissed out the decisive question. 'What did you do with our daughter?'

The grinning face knew he was getting his own small victory. He also knew if he turned the screw a bit more, the old woman with the gun might be so distraught she'd forget she was holding a weapon, and he could lunge his way to freedom.

It might have been half a plan, but Adde still didn't realise who he was dealing with. He did realise there was only one way to make-or-break the situation, so he took it.

He answered the question, lifting his eyes to the ceiling like he was recalling fond memories.

'Yeah, I remember Celia. She was the last one. Pretty gal, even if she was out of it most of the time. She went to a new life in the sun, if I remember right.'

'Where is she, you lowlife scum?'

'Aw, come on lady. Your daughter didn't seem to think I was. From what I remember she couldn't wait to get butt naked and snuggle in the sack with a bit of black.'

It was the final straw for Daisy. It could also have been a step too far for Adde, but as it turned out it was probably the best thing he could have done. For himself.

Daisy pulled the trigger. Emotions that had already been close to boiling point finally spilled over, and only her trigger finger was going to turn off the gas. She fired five quick shots, doing the one thing she really didn't need to do.

Chapter 30

Adde Wambua was nothing if not quick and nimble. Daisy might have lost control of her trigger finger, but she didn't lose it completely. She knew if she shot him dead, Celia's whereabouts would go to the grave with him.

She fired to miss, but in the split-second she had to react, she didn't take into account where he was standing.

As the five bullets whizzed around him they didn't take him out, but they took out the window right behind him. Both Daisy and Aidan froze in shock as the toughened glass of the double-glazed window disintegrated into a million jewels of crackling glass.

But Adde Wambua, no stranger to making quick escapes, didn't freeze. He looked behind him, and realized his escape hatch had inadvertently opened. He didn't hesitate, literally dived through the glassless frame, and rolled over onto the gravel of the drive to break his fall.

He ran for his life, heading like a hundred-metre runner for the gate. Then Daisy's disbelieving eyes caught a flash of black and white, running to block his route to freedom.

Sarah didn't stand a chance. The desperate fast-moving figure threw his arms out in front of him, and she was skittled out of the way, catapulted into the bushes like a rag doll. As Daisy and Aidan finally unfroze themselves, the last sight they had of him was watching him leap the gate, and disappear into the night.

They ran out of the side door, and knelt down next to a stunned Sarah, only just visible beneath the bushes. *'Sarah...'*

She looked like she didn't know where she was for a moment. '*Hell...* now I know what it feels like to be run over by a bus...' she mumbled weakly.

'Get her out,' said Aidan, slipping an arm around her back as Daisy did the same around her legs. Together they eased her onto the lawn, laid her out flat.

'What hurts?' said a fraught Daisy.

'Everything. But my boobs are flatter than they used to be,' she gasped as she sucked in the air that had just been ripped out of her lungs.

'You need to be checked over,' said Aidan.

She sat up slowly. 'I'm ok... I think. Just winded.'

'What were you thinking? He's twice as big as you.'

She extracted a twig from her blonde hair. 'I wasn't thinking. I just needed to stop him getting away. But... we need to call Burrows, get him picked up.'

Daisy was getting her thoughts back in line. 'No, we have to let him go. He was just about to tell us where Celia was, when...'

'You lost it?' said Aidan.

Daisy closed her eyes for a moment. 'Yeah, when I lost it. If you were the one with the gun, wouldn't you?'

He wrapped a hand around hers. 'Yes, I would. But I might not have shot to miss, so perhaps you were the right person to have a finger on the trigger three minutes ago.'

'Nice of you to say so, dear. But not quite accurate. I gave him his get-out-of-jail-free card, didn't I?'

'Guys, I really think we should involve the police now.'

Daisy shook her head, even though she knew they really should. 'Sarah, I know it's the right thing to do, but for Aidan and me it's the wrong thing.'

'Yes, I know. If he gets arrested now he'll clam up, and you'll never know where Celia is. I get that, but...'

'Please let us handle it, for one more day?'

'You said that yesterday.'

'Did I?'

Sarah shook a resigned head. 'So what's your genius plan now?'

'Get you inside, so we can check you over, and avoid the nosy-neighbour scenario.'

Sarah lay on Daisy's bed, topless apart from an almost non-existent bra. As Daisy felt around for any signs of broken ribs, she couldn't help the same feelings of familiarity sweeping through her already-fraught emotions.

Even half-naked, Sarah was still the image of Celia.

'Was she like me... inside I mean?'

Daisy nodded. 'In so many ways. If she hadn't... succumbed, she could have been anything she wanted. She was on her way to being a criminal lawyer, before...'

'Briggs?'

'She was spirited, strong-willed, just like you. She did daft things, just like you.'

'She sounds a bit like her mother then.'

'Can't disagree there. I think she dabbled in drugs at uni, although she never admitted it to her strict mother. It never got to be a problem then though, at least not one we noticed. But I guess if you get the taste for it, it never leaves you totally. When Briggs got his teeth into her, it couldn't have been too difficult to get her where he wanted her.'

'That's one difference between us. I never have, and never would tough the stuff.'

Daisy nodded sadly. 'I blame myself. I was retired, but my training should have taught me to recognise the signs before I did. Before it was too late...'

Sarah saw the gloss of tears in Daisy's eyes. 'Hey, it's far easier to see it in others, rather than admit to yourself those you love need help.'

'Is it?'

'Yes. Because when those in your family hit the wrong side of the tracks, most of us pretend it's not happening at first because we put the blame on ourselves.'

'You've a wise head on those young shoulders, Sarah.'

'I know. Even though you don't listen to it half the time.'

'Maybe, but I do appreciate it.' Daisy stood up, smiled. 'There's nothing broken that I can see. But your boobs will be sore tomorrow.'

'They're not exactly pain-free now.'

'Come on... let's see if Aidan has made that coffee yet, and find you a couple of nuclear-level painkillers.'

Just before Sarah headed home, Daisy's phone rang. She looked at it curiously. It was a number she didn't recognise, and the time had almost reached eleven in the evening. She answered, flicked it to speaker.

'Hello Flora, it's Irene. I'm sorry to ring you so late, but you did say to let you know. Henri has just got back. He seemed in a bit of a hurry, and he tried to slip in quietly, but not much gets past me!'

'Good of you to ring me, Irene. Thank you for letting me know.'

Sarah was gesticulating in the background. 'What shall we do?'

Daisy wasn't sure what to do, but then Irene made the decision for her.

'Wait... something's happening.' There was a pause, likely while she looked to see what the something was. *'I just heard a door slam, so I looked out over the forecourt.*

My window gives me a view of it. He's just thrown his case into the Rolls, and now he's driving out. What do you want me to do, Flora?'

Daisy shook her head. 'Say good riddance, Irene. You won't see him again. But thank you for letting me know.'

Sarah narrowed her eyes. 'I would say we can notify the ports to stop him getting away, but I guess that's not what you want, is it?'

'No dear. We failed this time, but if he's arrested now, that'll be it for finding Celia. We do have an extradition treaty with Belgium, right?'

'Yes, of course. But what are you saying, Daisy?'

'I'm saying this isn't over yet. However this plays out, it's going to have to do so on Belgian soil.'

Sarah headed home, without Daisy telling her exactly how it was going to play out. She didn't know exactly how herself, but she knew that somehow she still had to get Adde to tell her the rest of what he knew before she made sure the authorities got their teeth into him.

He and the Rolls were heading back to Belgium, and it was pretty clear what his plans had been. Finish what he'd started, and when he'd committed murder once again, get back to Belgium straight away. His ferry passage would already have been booked before he turned up at the cottage, unaware Daisy was already at the manor.

Carmella deBruin had made the journey the previous day, so that implicating her would be difficult, even though she'd given the order for Adde to fix his mistake on the way to the docks. Yet again he'd failed, and his mistress wasn't going to be too pleased. But epic failure or not, they both knew they'd be safer with him on Belgian soil.

The fly in the ointment was Adde's past, with a sting in its tail called Daisy, who had a very good reason to not let things lie.

Time was running out for Daisy to act, and she knew it. When Irene had called, for a moment she'd considered heading over to the manor to finish what she'd started. But then Adde and the Rolls had left, killing that particular plan stone dead.

Sarah wasn't going to listen to her pleas to hold off official intervention for any longer than another day. Adde was a murderer, and his mistress as good as, and as far as the police were concerned they both had to be brought to justice.

Daisy had twenty-four hours to come up with a way to get Adde to tell her what he knew, and put it into action, before he was arrested and kept his gob shut forever.

Aidan finished fixing thick cardboard at the smashed window, and just after midnight they crawled exhausted into bed, secure in the knowledge the man most likely to break in was already heading out of the country.

As they spooned each other to sleep, Daisy could still feel her heart racing. She'd been so close to discovering Celia's whereabouts, but lost her cool just at the wrong moment. She'd messed up, tipped over the edge by the words of a thug which might or might not be true.

But whatever the truth, she was getting the feeling she'd been played just as much as she'd played him. His devious mind had seen she was getting wound up, known if he'd said the right things some kind of endgame would have ensued. He'd played his last risky card, and it had won him the game.

Now Daisy had one last card to play. The problem was she couldn't see exactly what card it was, or how to play it.

She just knew that however low in the deck it was, it had to be played very quickly, or it wouldn't be put on the table at all.

Chapter 31

'How do you fancy a trip to Belgium, dear?'

Aidan had woken to find himself alone in bed, and padded downstairs to find Daisy glued to the computer screen in the office. He groaned inside at her question, but forced a smile onto his face.

'And what do you think we'll achieve by that, Flower?' he mumbled the question, all too aware her mind only had one track right then.

Her face clouded into indecision. 'To be honest I don't know yet. But we have to do something, before Sarah brings in the big guns.'

He couldn't help a grin. 'Didn't you do that yesterday? If I remember right, your big gun helped our only lead to escape.'

She reached out, took his hand. He felt her hand tremble a little as she squeezed a little comfort out of his. 'I know. I messed up, dear. But you heard what the slimeball said. Truth or otherwise, it tipped me into doing the worst thing I could have done. So now I have to put it right.'

'By walking into the lion's den without a protective suit?'

'Maybe. But Adde Wambua has to finish what he started. If that means risking my life, then so be it. But I can't ask you to do the same. If I have to go on my own, I will.'

He shook his head. 'This is our daughter we're talking about, dear. I don't have a choice, even if I wanted one.'

'Do you want one?'

He kissed her gently. 'No, I don't. How do we get there?'

'It's already booked. Three o'clock this afternoon, direct flight from Southend.'

'So what if I'd said no?'

She grinned. 'This is our daughter we're talking about, Dip.'

He shook his head, and then had a sudden thought. 'We've got no front window glass... we can't go away with cardboard instead of double-glazing.'

'That's sorted too. The emergency glazier is coming this afternoon. When you've made me Welsh Rarebit, I'll pop and see if Maisie will look after him for us, and then we'd better pack an overnight bag and get going.'

He shook his head again, and then headed to the kitchen.

'Daisy, what happened?'

'I threw something at Aidan, missed him but it went through the window instead.'

Maisie raised her eyebrows. 'That's not like you, Daisy. Well, it is... but you know what I mean.'

'I'm kidding. We were playing rap music too loud, it shattered the glass.'

'Really?'

'No, Maisie. Aidan had a bit of an accident with a hammer, that's all.'

'Now you are pulling my chain.'

Daisy groaned to herself. Her dotty friend would rather believe either of the first two options than the one half-reasonable explanation. 'Does it really matter, Maisie? Can you be there at three for the glazier of not?'

'Of course, dear. I'll take Brutus for a walk at the same time. Are you sure everything is alright?'

'I'm fine, Maisie,' Daisy lied. 'Just a little stressed. Family trouble, you know.'

'If you want to share, I'm there for you.'

152

Daisy politely declined, telling Maisie the truth that she and Aidan had to get going. It was mid-morning, and they needed to be on the road. No one in the village knew they even had a daughter, and for the time being, that was the way it had to stay.

Whether that would ever change was anybody's guess.

Aidan already had the bags in the car when she got back. Five minutes later they were on the road to Southend. It would take longer to get there than the flight to Antwerp, but if they missed it there wouldn't be another one until tomorrow.

And tomorrow was a day too late.

They caught the flight. It seemed like they'd only just taken off and settled back in their seats before the aeroplane was descending again, the entire flight taking just an hour.

The late-afternoon sun was heading south as they walked through the airport lobby, and were met just outside by a middle-aged man with an oversized moustache, and hair that was just turning silver at the edges. He was wearing a long, light-brown coat, and a red tartan scarf dangled around his neck.

Once, way back, Daisy had known him well, but she hadn't seen him for over twenty years. They'd kept in touch, exchanging an annual email every New Year.

'Felix...' She gave him a hug, introduced him to Aidan, who he'd never had cause to meet before.

His deceptively-jovial face looked a little concerned, as he spoke in a Belgian accent. 'Forgive me Daisy; it is so good to see you after all this time, but your request was a little surprising, to say the least.'

153

'And just between us of course, Felix?'

'Of course. My superiors would not condone such a thing, if they ever found out.'

'My dear friend, I can't tell you a lot. Just suffice it to say we crossed paths with someone who very likely knows where Celia is, and I need the... tools to persuade him to tell me, and I would have never got them through customs.'

He raised bushy eyebrows. 'So you have discovered she is still alive, yes?'

'It would seem that way. But she's very probably not living either... not as we know it anyway. I have to find her, Felix. If there was any other way...'

He put a hand on her arm. 'Say no more, dear lady. Perhaps the less I know of this, the better.'

'You always were an understanding man, Felix.'

He laughed jovially, and led them through the main car park into a much smaller one for short-term visitors. He glanced around to make sure no prying eyes were watching, and opened the boot lid of a red Alfa Romeo Spider, and pulled out a long thin sports bag, which didn't contain anything that could be called sporting.

Daisy checked inside it, and nodded her approval. 'How many cartridges, Felix?'

'More than you need. Please be careful. You are telling me little of your quest, so that actually tells me a lot, my dear friend.'

'Thank you for not quizzing me, Felix.'

He laughed again. 'Oh Daisy, my dear, if I thought it would get me anywhere, I would fire a barrage of questions at you. But if experience of our dealings in the past is anything to go on, I would only get what you decided I needed to know.'

154

'Back in the day, that was only when it wouldn't be good for your health to know.'

'And now?' he grinned.

'Now it wouldn't be good for your employment, Felix.'

'No matter. But I am here for you... just a phone call away, please remember that.'

'I won't forget. But on the subject of being here for me... we really could do with a lift, if you've a half-hour to spare?'

Chapter 32

Sarah pulled into the drive at the cottage. It was almost four in the afternoon, and she was getting concerned. The gate was open, and the first thing she noticed was the glazier's van parked in the drive.

The second thing she noticed was Brutus, tied to a tree trunk by his red lead. She shook her head as she climbed out of the car, but the cat-cum-dog looked quite happy, sitting obediently in the late-afternoon sunshine with his paws out in front of him like a sphinx guarding a tomb.

She'd called Daisy's phone a few hours ago, to check she was doing okay after her altercation with Adde. There had been no answer. She'd called every hour after that, each time getting the same *this mobile phone is switched off* message.

She'd tried Aidan's phone, got the same message. The house phone rang out, unanswered. And with each unanswered call, the dull ache of dread in her gut had worsened. The previous night Daisy had refused to say what was in her mind, other than the fact she had to take quick action.

Sarah doubted that last night even Daisy herself had known what that action was to be, but the dull ache wasn't exactly unfounded, and well and truly based on previous bitter experience.

She was getting to know her new friend a lot better. And one of the things she was starting to realise was that where her daughter's welfare was concerned, Daisy's crazy streak went into another galaxy altogether.

But the rapidly-building fear of the probably-inevitable had got too much, so a short while ago she'd jumped in a police car, and driven the fifteen miles to Great Wiltingham. It was beginning to look like she'd been deliberately excluded from Daisy's hastily-formed plans, and that wasn't sitting easily at all. There was only one way to find out.

A slightly-portly woman appeared in the front porch, dressed entirely in polyester and wearing a concerned frown on her face. Sarah was in uniform, and a blue-and-yellow had just turned into the drive.

'Um... can I help you?' the woman said nervously, trying to smile.

Sarah knew who she was. The furball tied to the tree meant her reputation had preceded her. 'I'm Officer Lowry. You must be Maisie.'

The woman looked horrified. 'Oh dear... don't tell me I have mug-shots on file? Have I done something wrong?'

Sarah tried to smile reassuringly. 'No, Maisie. I'm a friend of Daisy's. I was just passing.'

'Oh, thank goodness for that.' She slapped a hand across her chest, like she was trying to restart her heart. 'For a moment there I thought maybe Aidan's antics with the hammer had been more... drastic than Daisy said.'

'I'm sorry?'

Maisie flicked both arms out, and grinned coyly. 'Oh, don't mind me, dear. My dotty mind runs away with me sometimes.'

Sarah smiled again, a little more sympathetically that time. 'What are you doing here, Maisie? Are Daisy and Aidan not here?'

'No dear. They're away for a couple of days.' She indicated the glazier working away at the bay. 'Daisy asked me to see to the repairs while they were gone.'

The dull ache in Sarah's stomach suddenly grew more acute. 'Gone away? Did she say where?'

'Belgium apparently. Don't ask me why though, I can't imagine what's in Belgium that's in any way interesting.'

'Oh, I can.'

'Really dear?'

'Um... how long have they been gone, Maisie?'

'Oh, hours. Catching the three o'clock flight from Southend. Are they running away, dear? I know I shouldn't ask.'

'Oh they're running alright. But not away as such. More like *to* somewhere.'

'Oh I say. Are they fugitives from something? It's all very mysterious.'

Sarah put a hand on Maisie's arm, realising if she wasn't careful there would be a remake of *The Fugitive* if Maisie's overactive imagination had anything to do with it. Mysterious facts that seemed to defy logical explanation weren't helping, so she had to nip it in the bud before it took over the village.

'Please don't think either Daisy or Aidan have done anything illegal,' she said, cringing inside at the only-just truth. 'I'm sure they have just gone for a quick break, to... help mend Aidan's flattened finger.'

She cringed inside again, but somehow Maisie seemed to gel with her slightly-crazy explanation. 'That makes sense, dear. Shall I tell them you called in, if they phone?'

'No... please don't. I mean... no, I'll call Daisy myself later. It might be best if you just make sure the window is secure before nightfall?'

'Oh yes dear, I can do that. Just give Daisy my love if you speak to her before I do!'

158

Sarah drove back to the station, knowing there was no way Maisie would get through to Daisy. Knowing there was no way she would either, not until Daisy had either achieved her objectives or died trying. The severe pain in her gut was stabbing a sharp reminder either of those options were distinctly possible.

Daisy had deliberately slipped out of the country without telling her. The fact both their phones were off was a confirmation they were up to something her official career wouldn't approve of.

She knew why. Whatever insanity they were planning was driven by an all-consuming need to know what had happened to their daughter. Which was closely followed by a need to keep her out of the equation, for two obvious reasons.

Daisy knew all too well that this time Sarah would stop her doing what the rest of the world saw as sheer insanity. Her slightly-insane friend was aware how dangerous it was, and even if Sarah went along with holding off official action, knew she would insist on being there to help protect her friend.

Daisy wasn't going to allow anyone except Aidan to accompany her into the Belgian lioness's lair. Slipping away before Sarah knew what was happening was the only way.

She thumped the steering wheel with frustration. Then she swallowed hard to get her emotions under control, and glanced at her watch. It was almost five. The flight to Antwerp couldn't be much more than an hour, so they'd already be in Belgium, and quite possibly close to the deBruin mansion.

She'd promised Daisy to give her another day before involving Burrows. Sarah lifted her head momentarily to the

159

roof of the car, cried out her anguish. She'd almost kept her promise, but not quite.

As she drove through the suburbs of Kings Lynn, heading quickly to the station, she knew she couldn't keep quiet any more. It might well be too late to stop the inevitable happening, but she had to try.

Chapter 33

Felix dropped Daisy and Aidan a few hundred yards down from the entrance to the baroque mansion, next to an imposing fortress-style twelve-foot high stone wall. She gave him a quick hug, and he drove away with a cheery but slightly-nervous wave.

Aidan shouldered the Slazenger bag, and they set off for the short walk to the entrance.

'So what's the plan, Rambo?' he said.

'I prefer Hetty.'

'Who?'

'Never mind, dear. She's my favourite character in a fictitious American police drama. But you don't need your galactic-sized brain to work out what the plan is. We just seek out Adde, and persuade him to tell us where Celia is.'

'Sounds simple when you put it like that. Even my brain can work that out. But like the most simple of plans, there's a lot of complicated side-effects that can spin it out of control.'

'Course there is. We need to find out where he is, and then terrify the hell out of him. The last bit shouldn't be difficult, I shot at him before so he knows I've got an itchy trigger finger.'

'You... um, did fire to miss, I assume?'

'Dear, you know me better than that. If I'd shot to kill, the answer to the question we need would never have been given. He is very likely the only person on the planet who can answer it, after all.'

'Yes, and he might well be aware of that.'

'That's a bridge we cross when we come to it.'

161

He suddenly pulled her to one side. They were ten feet away from the main entrance, and he'd spotted the heavy iron gates and the sentry-box right next to them. 'We're never going to get in that way. Especially not carrying tennis rackets.'

Daisy glanced back the way they'd come. 'Bugger, as you'd say, dear. Seems like the lady of the mansion likes her privacy. You think this wall goes all the way around the perimeter?'

'Only one way to find out.'

They retraced their steps. It was starting to get dark, and while the darkness was likely to be their friend, it wasn't exactly helping to search for a way in that no one else used. The stone wall seemed to go on for miles, but it was only a couple of hundred yards from where Felix had dropped them when it turned a right-angle.

A narrow footpath branched off the country lane next to it, looked like it followed the wall. It was dark and forbidding, and somewhat overgrown, but there was little choice other than to follow it. The ground beneath their feet was muddy and slippery, and the footpath seemed to go on for another age, but then it filtered into a second, narrower lane, and the wall turned ninety degrees again.

They followed the lane, which nestled the wall and sloped downhill a little. Then the welcome solidity of asphalt turned into a narrow grassy track. They could smell the sea.

Now there were tall bushes between them and the wall. They kept going, and then the track opened out into a bigger space. It looked like an old, disused boatyard. A few rotting hulks of old fishing boats sat on the higher ground, and an old corrugated-iron shack looked like the next storm would raze it to the ground.

There wasn't a soul around. It looked like no one had been there for years.

They trekked across the open ground, found themselves looking at a rickety old wooden quay. In the gloom of the distance, they could just about make out the low hills of the Dutch side of the estuary, almost two miles away.

Daisy glanced to her right. Just before the wooden quay, the bushes had petered out, and the high perimeter wall of the chateau was easy to see. The wall stretched right to the water's edge, but its last few feet had been exposed to the elements and had crumbled, some of the rocks the stonemasons had used to build it a couple of centuries ago laying in random piles at its base.

The water was just lapping around them, forming man-made rock pools in the high tide. But for Daisy, it was a way in. She pointed to the end of the wall. 'What do you think, Dip?'

'We'll get wet feet.'

'We're about to walk right in to the lion's den, and that's what concerns you?'

'Course not. Just an observation, dear. Let's go.'

As it turned out, they only got slightly-damp feet. The piles of rectangular rocks acted like stepping-stones, and there was only a couple of places where they had to grasp the end of the wall and hang on for dear life like they were climbing Everest. Aidan dropped a foot into a rock pool, but other than that, with a lot of grunting and groaning from them both, they made the other side of the wall without incident.

A mass of ornamental bushes tried to spear them to death as they fought their way through the branches in the virtual darkness. But they were no match for two intrepid, determined explorers who had little idea what they'd find around the next bush.

But as they stumbled out of the undergrowth onto lush, manicured lawns, what they found stopped them in their tracks for a moment or two.

Daisy shook a disparaging head as her eyes followed the gently-sloping lawns to the house in the distance.

'Wow... how the other Belgian half live, hey dear?'

Chapter 34

Sarah found Burrows in his office, pouring over papers from the CPS relating to Finlay Finnegan's prosecution. He looked up as she knocked on his door, beckoned her to enter.

'Lowry... mind telling me where you've been?'

She swallowed hard. There was no way to say words that wouldn't incur his wrath, so there was nothing for it but to tell him the truth. Most of it anyway.

'I have reason to believe that two of our elderly citizens are in danger, sir.'

His expression switched into a mixture of despair and resignation. 'I assume I don't need to ask which two, Officer?'

'You don't need to ask, no.'

He buried his face in his hands. 'That woman will be the death of me.'

'If we don't act, sir, it could very likely be the death of her.'

He groaned. 'What has she done now?'

Sarah gave him a nutshell version of recent history, leaving out any mention of secret DNA tests and shattered windows. She did include a run-down of what it was *really* about, making sure he was aware of the reasons why Daisy and Aidan were so determined to confront the man they believed was responsible for the murder they'd drawn a blank investigating.

She knew if he believed that once again Daisy could make the Norfolk police appear more efficient than they actually were, he would take the situation more seriously.

She needed him to take action, and there was no better motivation than having something in it for him.

He slapped his hands to his face again, but then peeped at her through parted fingers. He was a jaded, battle-weary DCI, old enough to believe men made far better cops than women, but he'd managed to retain a sense of right and wrong through it all.

'So you're telling me that...um, two of our senior citizens are about to walk into a life-threatening situation, in a *foreign country*?'

'I believe so, sir. And I'm seriously concerned, given their extreme motivation.'

He groaned in a resigned kind of way. 'So am I, Lowry. Despite the wrecking ball of frustration making me want to lock them up and throw away the key for their own protection...and ours. But we can't just go swanning into Belgium without official cooperation from the Belgian police, or there'll be hell to pay.'

Sarah was about to beg him to get permission, but he'd already picked up the phone.

'Get me the chief of police in Antwerp.'

Sarah lowered her head. 'Thank you, sir,' she said quietly.

He shook his head. 'Now *you'll* be the death of me, Lowry. But despite the fact most of you young guns see me as a dinosaur, I wouldn't forgive myself if anything happened to those two... pests.'

The phone jingled. 'Yes? DCI Burrows here.'

'Ah, Inspecteur... Pierre Richelau here, chief of police in Antwerp. You have just caught me. I am about to leave, to put on my finery for the ambassador's ball this evening. So please make it quick. What can I do for you?'

166

Burrows groaned inside. The man sounded impatient, and not as receptive as he could have done. 'I'm sorry to disturb you, sir. But we have reason to believe two... elderly UK citizens are in Antwerp, and in grave danger.'

'I see. Do you know their whereabouts?'

'Yes. They are located at Carmella deBruin's mansion.'

The voice hesitated. *'Come, Inspecteur, if they are enjoying Mrs. deBruin's hospitality at the chateau, I can assure you they are in no danger.'*

'With all due respect sir, we have further reason to believe she is harbouring a suspected murderer.'

'Mon Dieu... you English police, always thinking the worst. You do not understand, monsieur, Carmella is a fine, well-respected citizen. She would not do such a thing. You are mistaken.'

Sarah threw her hands in the air. 'Thinking the worst? Belgian apathy rules again?'

Burrows wasn't giving up that easily. 'Sir, are you saying you cannot help us?'

'Listen to me, Inspecteur... we have already imposed on her, against my wishes, when your drugs squad suspected she was involved with her son's misdemeanours. We were embarrassed to find nothing to incriminate her, as I already knew we wouldn't. I was forced to grovel an apology. Mrs. deBruin is a patron of justice here, held in high respect by the lawful community. The chateau is a fortress, no one can get in unless they are invited. And tonight, she is to attend the ball as a special guest. So you expect me to crash in on a false suspicion, yet again? Tonight of all nights?'

'We believe it is more than a false suspicion, sir.'

'Then once again you are mistaken, Inspecteur.' They heard him let out a deep, impatient sigh. *'However, I will*

instruct a patrol car to drive by in the next hour, and look out for anything out of the ordinary.'

'That's it?' cried Sarah. Burrows waved to her to button it. 'Sir, if you won't do anything, do we have your permission to come to Antwerp in an official capacity?'

'If you wish to waste your time and resources, Inspecteur, I will not stop you coming. But you do not have my permission to enter the chateau, or disturb Mrs. deBruin in any way. Now I must go, so I will bid you goodnight.'

The phone clicked off. Sarah turned a full circle in sheer frustration. 'He's in league with her,' she cried.

A slight smile broke across Burrow's face. 'I doubt he's actually that, but she's got him in her pocket. When you're rich enough, anyone is fair game.'

'It stinks.'

'Surely does. But it doesn't make our job any easier, to say the least.'

'So what do we do now?'

He shook his head despairingly. 'Much against my better judgement, we'd better get over there, do what we can. We could be too late, but it seems if we don't do something about it, no one else will.'

'Thank you, sir,' Sarah breathed.

'Don't thank me. Those two infuriating pains-in-my-neck have kind of forced my hand... with a little kick up the ass from you. Just go home and get your passport, right now.'

Sarah headed to the door, but then the phone jingled again. Burrows answered it. 'DCI Burrows.'

The voice on the other end sounded French-Dutch too. *'Forgive me for calling, Inspector. It is Felix Marchant, Belgian SIS. One of your citizens is in trouble, I believe. I promised her I would keep the secret, but I grow too concerned.'*

168

'Let me guess... Daisy Henderson?'

'Yes, yes. How did you know?'

'Let's just say she is known to us. In fact, we are just about to leave for Antwerp... although the Belgian police are being no help whatsoever.'

'It is no surprise to me. That is why I called you. I do not know what to do. Without clear evidence we cannot intervene. Do you know something I don't?'

'You likely know more than we do, Felix. One of my officers who is acquainted with them has grown seriously worried, with good reason. We're on our way, but it will be several hours.'

'We might not have hours, my friend. Daisy contacted me, and I picked them up from the airport, dropped them outside the deBruin chateau. I am aware of their personal situation, which just makes me even more worried.'

'Yeah, me too, Felix. Give me your number, we'll call you when we're close.'

'I'll drive by the chateau, but I can do little else officially. This is far from an official operation. Please get here as quick as you can, or I fear the worst.'

Chapter 35

'It's like a mini version of Ely Cathedral!'

Daisy's slightly-breathless exclamation wasn't that far from the truth. The gently-sloping manicured lawns stretched three hundred yards to a long terrace that fronted the rear of the main house. A mass of square windows were interspersed with tall, thin gothic turrets that seemed to spear into the air like angry needles.

The pale-yellow rear wall of the house was topped with a steep-angled roof of dark grey slate, which just added to the ominous and eloquent baroque feel of the chateau. Pointed dormer windows gave a little light to the third-floor rooms, set into the huge roof that looked just as big as the wall itself. Each dormer was topped with a small turret, confirming the feeling the chateau was more like a medieval castle than a cosy residence.

Over to their left, a long wooden landing stage stretched a little way into the estuary. Lit by low, more modern lamps, a small American-style fishing cruiser sat moored to the end, at the part of the quay that always had a depth of water, even at low tide.

An elegant, ancient boathouse sat a little nearer to the house, set to one side of the landing stage, and served by a concrete slipway that would be under water at high tide. Beyond that, a long, low building with more windows and a clock-tower in the centre of its roof seemed to be built off one side of the terrace.

'Do you think that's the servant's quarters?' said Aidan.

'Stands a good chance. But we need to see the rest of the place, find out how the land lies.'

They crept along the side of the wall, heading closer to the house. Some of the windows had light behind their drapes, but no one seemed to be around. There was no way to know where their target was, or even whether he was in the main house or the servant's quarters.

As they reached the low stone wall separating the terrace from the lawn, Daisy paused. 'Knowing what Adde's duties were, if you can call them that, he might be... otherwise occupied in the main house, if you get me.'

'My huge brain tells me he might not even be here. His mistress is likely well pissed off with him for failing to kill you twice now. Maybe he's cleared off to pastures new.'

'Hmm... I don't think so. He left the UK with that super-expensive Rolls Royce, remember? I doubt Carmella would take that lying down if he cleared off with it. And epic fail or not, he knows where his bread is buttered. He won't give that up easily.'

'Well there's one way to find out. If the Rolls is here, then he likely is too.'

'Galactic brain kicking in, dear?'

'Hardly. Even you could have worked that one out.'

'I'll ignore that. Retribution sometime in the near future.'

They crept around the corner of the terrace, heading for the front of the house. The chateau was so wide, there was just thirty feet of space between its side and the stone perimeter wall. It was dark there, but the house was a lot narrower than it was wide, and the front gardens they couldn't yet see seemed to be ablaze with light, helping them to see where they were going.

As they reached the front corner, Aidan pulled Daisy against the wall of the building. They gazed in an awesome kind of way at the landscaping that looked like it needed a small army of gardeners to keep maintained.

171

Bowling-green lawns stretched up and away from a large forecourt that looked like it belonged to a luxury hotel. Huge beds interspersed the grass, filled with ornamental bushes and flowering plants. Each one had a statue of some kind, probably figurines of the rich family who had owned the house for centuries.

Bright spotlights flooded each bed with carefully-positioned beams, bathing the whole two-acre frontage with diffused light, the brightness and shadows creating an illusion of an even bigger garden. More lights bathed the forecourt in brightness, looking like ancient European streetlights.

Some of them were bathing the Rolls Royce sitting there, the light bright enough for them to instantly recognise it.

'It looks like a James Bond villain's residence,' Daisy whispered.

'Isn't that almost what it is? Leaving the Dalmatians out of it, or course.'

'Funny guy...'

Daisy choked the words into silence, and slunk back against the corner of the house. The front door they couldn't see had opened, and someone walked out. He was dressed in formal chauffeur-wear, and opened the rear door of the Rolls, waiting for someone to join him.

It wasn't Adde Wambua.

Daisy glanced to Aidan. 'Are we going somewhere?' she whispered.

Someone was going somewhere. A vision in black and white appeared, dripping in diamonds that sparkled in the light of the lamps. The signature red stilettos trotted across the forecourt, and the long black dress enveloped by a pure white mid-length coat with a pure white fur collar dazzled the eyes of those trying to focus on it.

A diamond tiara seemed to compete for the dazzle stakes, visible for just for a few seconds before she slipped into the elegant darkness of the rear seat, and the light show was over. The chauffeur dropped into the driving seat, and the Rolls headed up the meandering, sloping drive, to the heavy iron gates that opened for the car, and then closed again as it disappeared from view.

'Where's she going?' said Daisy.

'Even my galactic-sized brain can't answer that, dear. But there's some kind of function going on, seeing as she's brought out the bling. And it looks like our thug might be out of favour after all.'

'You don't think she's... let him go?'

Aidan shook his head, unsure. 'It's a possibility. If she has, it could well be that our trip was in vain. But I'm hoping he's too valuable in... other ways. If that's the case, he's just been demoted rather than fired.'

'That might mean he's also been demoted from the main house. Maybe we should explore the servant's quarters. There's no other buildings here at the front, it's too public for her posh friends. So that block we saw is for sure the servant's domain. I think we should start there... and it's single-storey too, unlike Ely Cathedral.'

'Lead the way, Rambo.'

'Will you stop calling me that? He's older than I am now!'

Chapter 36

Daisy and Aidan slunk back to the rear of the house, and then slunk doubled over along the lawn side of the terrace wall, making sure if anyone looked out of a window they wouldn't be seen. As far as anyone knew, Carmella deBruin lived alone, her baroque estate inhabited by far more staff than owners.

Even so, most of them were probably loyal to their mistress, despite the fact they were likely treated like scum. Being spotted by a member of the service team was for sure going to be bad for their health.

They made it to the corner of the servant's block. Daisy looked along the lawn-side wall; there were several square windows, a few of them with lights on, sending out shafts of brightness across the dark grass.

'Let's sneak a look in the ones we can.'

They edged along the side wall, peering into each window that had light emanating from it. Their eyes fell on several staff members, relaxing in their down time. It was gone eight in the evening, so most of them were done for the day.

None of them were Adde Wambua.

They reached the end of the long wall, edged around the short wall. 'Let's try the other side,' said Daisy.

The block was built right up against the perimeter wall, the country lane where Felix had dropped them off just the other side of it. There was only three feet of space to squeeze down. Once more, a few of the windows were blazing with light.

The first two didn't reveal anyone of interest. Then, as Daisy peeped over the cill of the third window, a smile broke over her face.

'*Jackpot,*' she breathed, more than a little relief in her tone.

The Nigerian was there, stretched out on his bed with his hands behind his shaved head, grinning as he watched some kind of comedy programme on his TV.

They counted the windows as they headed to the front of the building. It likely had a central walkway with doors off both sides of it. There was only one window between Adde's room and the front wall, so it wouldn't be difficult to know which door was his when they entered the building.

Daisy turned to Aidan. 'Give me your phone, please dear.'

He looked at her curiously. She switched it on, dialled Sarah's number as she smiled to Aidan. 'We'll see if we can get Adde on video, confessing to murder.'

'How...' he started to say, but then a frantic voice answered the call. '*Aidan... what the hell... why is your phone switched off, as if I didn't know. I've been peeing myself with worry here...*'

'Sarah, it's Daisy. We're fine, but there's no time to explain now. Kind of in the middle of something here. Have you got WhatsApp on your phone?'

'*What? Yes I have, but...*'

'Good. Then keep watching, coz I'm about to make a video call to you. It might be quite a long one, and if he realises what we're doing it might get cut off suddenly. But it'll be on your phone then, so it'll be too late. Modern technology, hey?'

'*Daisy? He?*'

'No time for explanations, dear.'

175

The voice grew stern. *'Daisy, we know where you are.'*

'What? How?'

'Both your phones were off, so I called in to the cottage. Maisie was there. She told me you'd gone away, and I didn't need Aidan's galactic-sized brain to work out where.'

Daisy groaned to herself. She'd had to involve Maisie because of the shattered window, but she'd not banked on Sarah actually turning up. 'Ok, we're at Carmella's chateau, and Adde Wambua is here too. We're just about to confront him, hence the imminent video call. Make sure you record it, ok?'

There was silence for a moment, apart from the sounds of the phone being handed over. Then another familiar voice barked out words. *'Daisy, don't you dare do anything idiotic until we get there. You hear me?'*

'Inspector? *Get there?* Where are you?'

'Heading to Mildenhall, catching a C-130 to Belgium, courtesy of a friend in the USAF. We're still a few hours away, so I'm ordering you to stay put until we get there.'

'Oh, Inspector... you seem to be breaking up... useless Belgian internet...' Daisy killed the call, shook her head. 'It seems our intrepid police force is on its way, dear.'

'Then we'd better go do what we have to before they get here, otherwise he'll never spill.'

'Agreed. You know what to do with that phone?'

'I do have a galactic-sized brain, remember?'

'Ok, then set it going now, while you can.'

He video-called Sarah, made sure the call had connected but didn't say anything in actual words. The Slazenger racket bag had a net pocket on one end, designed to hold drinks, so he slipped the phone into it with the screen facing out, so it was partly concealed. The netting would get in the way of a clear video, but it was better than nothing. The audio side was the most important after all, and the microphone would pick up what was said in Adde's room.

At least until he clocked what they were doing, which if they both crossed their fingers, might end up being a case of him shutting the stable door after the horse had bolted.

Daisy cringed as she spotted Sarah's frantic face on the screen behind the netting. Her young friend cried out, *'Daisy, don't do this...'*

'Sorry Sarah,' she said into the phone. 'But you know why we are. Now shut your gob, otherwise you'll give the game away.'

Sarah shut her gob reluctantly, stuck a silent finger up instead, all too aware if she kept talking, her friends would be in even more danger than they already were.

Daisy nodded to Aidan. 'Ok. She's got the message. Let's do this...'

The two of them clambered up onto the end of the terrace. The main door was in the centre of the front wall, accessed from the terrace paving.

'Let's hope no one gets itchy feet, comes out for a smoke or something.'

'His room is only a short way along. I suggest we just go for it, not hang about. Just walk straight into the passageway, and right through his doorway.'

Daisy nodded. She'd not intended hanging around any longer than necessary anyway. 'You got those tennis rackets ready for a game, dear?'

He nodded, put a hand on the shoulder strap.

'Then it's a go.'

They walked through the main door. A long, featureless walkway stretched in front of them, doors leading off it at regular intervals, like a corridor in a cheap hotel. Daisy

177

strode straight to the second door on the right, didn't bother knocking.

She already knew their target was relaxing on the bed, thinking he was as safe as chateaux. Just where she wanted him.

'Anyone for tennis, Adde?'

Chapter 37

He looked like his legs had suddenly self-combusted. In a nano-second he wrenched himself bolt upright on the bed, his big eyes like disbelieving saucers, his mouth gaping open inanely.

'You... geez... how..?'

Daisy had to grin, not just because of his shock, but the fact he'd been watching a comedy programme on the TV, and just at the perfect moment the studio audience had burst out laughing.

But Adde Wambua wasn't laughing anymore. As Aidan dropped the sports bag on his table with the net end facing into the room, Daisy whipped out the automatic rifle kindly provided by Felix, and aimed it at the still-frozen Nigerian.

'Good to see you, Adde,' she growled menacingly.

'You... hell, lady... you is like the friend who doesn't know when to piss off home...'

'You know what they say about us senior citizens, son. Always outstaying our welcome...'

'You ain't never spoken a truer word, old woman.'

She hitched back the firing chamber, glared into his big eyes. 'You call me that again and my itchy trigger finger will get a mind of its own. But this time I won't miss.'

The words seemed to sink in. 'Ok, ok... so we's all one big happy family again. So now what?'

'Oh Adde... you really don't get it, do you? You tried to do away with me, twice, and failed dismally both times. So now you owe me.'

'I... I was just carrying out orders, lady.'

'Orders? From who?'

'You know who. My boss... she don't take kindly to folks ruining her son's life.'

'You mean Carmella?'

'You stupid, girl? 'Course I mean Mrs. deBruin. I didn't have no choice if I wanted to keep my job. Nothin' personal, you get me?'

'Oh I get you. You still failed though. And now here I am, another vengeful woman giving you orders.'

'You ain't given me orders yet. Just pointed that thing at me.'

'As long as it brings back bad memories, Adde. So let me make it clear why we're really here. You know where our daughter is. So I'm ordering you to tell me.'

A slight, nervous smile spread across his face. 'Yeah... and I'm the only one who does know. So you ain't gonna shoot me, is you?'

Daisy groaned. She'd steered the conversation and got a video murder confession from him, but the real information they needed was going to be a lot harder to come by. He was just as aware of the harsh facts of life as they were.

'Ok, boy. You tell us what we want to know, and I won't shoot you. How's that for a deal?'

'Nah. Ain't no deal, lady. Especially as I got a couple of my boys comin' round any minute now... and they know how to use their assets, if you get me.'

Daisy snorted dismissively. 'Oh come on, Adde. That's the oldest trick in the book. An old pro like me is never going to fall for that.' She hitched the rifle tighter to her shoulder. *'So who did you sell my daughter to?'*

He grinned, his oversized white teeth barred in a confident sneer now he'd recovered his composure and realised what was what. 'That's for me to know, old girl,' he said, putting on a fake posh English accent.

180

'So you want me to wipe that idiotic smile off your face then?'

'Ain't gonna happen, lady.'

'You know what happens when you push me...'

For a second the smile faltered, the bad memories kicking in. And so did the uncertainty of not knowing if, back at her house, the lady with the gun had actually fired to miss or not. But then the sickly sneer was back.

'Hey, I ain't pushin' you, girl. Just refusing to give you any satisfaction. While you's pointing that thing at me anyway.'

Daisy lowered the gun, a little. The thug seemed way too confident, considering she'd thought she held all the cards and the big gun. Either he was taking a big risk with his life, or was totally brainless. Or maybe...

'Ok, you win. I'm not pointing a deadly weapon at you anymore. So now tell me what I want to know.'

Still he was grinning, like he'd scored a minor victory. Or maybe, was about to score a major victory.

Something happened. It had crossed Daisy's mind he was acting way more confidently that she'd expected, and suddenly she knew why. It might have been the oldest trick in the book, bur right then it happened to be true. The door burst open, and the two of his boys she'd thought were just figments of his imagination turned out to be all too real.

One of them, a white guy, was carrying a big bag of McDonald's fast food. The other, a black guy, saw what was happening, and in less than a second whipped out a handgun.

Adde, the sick grin just about as wide as it could possibly get, waved an introductory hand into the air. 'See, you old has-beens, I told you. Say hello to my squad.'

181

Chapter 38

The black guy wrenched the rifle out of Daisy's hands. 'We going to trash these old fogies now, Henri?'

Aidan thought quickly. Still standing deliberately next to the sports bag, he reached into the net pocket and killed the video call. The screen went black. Adde had been so wrapped up in his own personal fall and rise of Reginald Perrin, he hadn't had the time to notice he'd been recorded.

The man himself had been thinking quickly too. 'You kidding me, Denz? My boss, she don't like *murder* on the premises. And if we do them in now, there ain't no proof I's redeemed myself.'

'So what we gonna do then?'

Adde grinned menacingly again. 'That washed-up old has-been ain't got her weapon anymore, so they's both helpless. They ain't no threat now, so when Carmella gets back we go see her, then she can decide what we do with them. She'll be here in an hour or so, gets bored with them official functions quick. And we got food to eat, and then fish to catch!'

'Sounds like a plan to me.'

Denzil wrenched open the sports bag, saw there was nothing else in there other than spare magazines, and then Adde threw the bag onto the bed together with its owners.

'Sit there, and don't try anything pointless.'

The three thugs gathered at the table, the gun on one end, and burgers, fries and large cokes in polystyrene cups with thick straws poking out of their tops filling the rest of the tabletop. The TV was still blaring out the comedy programme Adde had been watching, but for Daisy the studio laughter didn't seem funny anymore.

The joke had shifted, well and truly onto the other foot.

Their captors seemed to be enjoying their food. Daisy glanced to Aidan, and he saw the mist of defeat in her eyes, wrapped a consoling arm around her shoulders and pulled her tight into him. He was just as aware as she that Adde had implicated himself and his mistress in her attempted murder, but right then things weren't exactly looking positive for resolving the main reason they were there, or doing anything to prevent her real murder.

Adde was all too right. They *were* helpless. The gun was twelve feet away, the wrong side of three young and fit thugs who clearly didn't have much of a conscience when it came to doing what they deemed necessary.

And now the one person who could tell them where Celia was didn't have the slightest intention of sharing that information.

The food was gone. Adde stood up, glanced at his watch, and took another draw on his coke straw. 'It's almost ten, guys. Carmella will be back any time now. We should get these old cronies into the house ready for when she arrives.'

Daisy and Aidan were bundled out of the room, Aidan slinging the sports bag over his shoulder as they were shoved along the corridor and out onto the terrace. No one bothered that he was carrying it, all three of them knowing there was nothing in it that was a threat to anyone.

On that one they were wrong. As they were led through double leaded conservatory doors into the house, he fumbled with the phone in the net pocket, managed to connect a video call to a fraught Sarah, and silently rested his arm over the screen so no one could see it was on.

He and Daisy were led through an elegant, high-ceilinged rear hall, and through into an equally-luxurious sitting room. Adde threw all the lights on, which included a lamp standing on a large, Queen-Anne table on one side of the room.

Aidan nonchalantly dropped the bag onto it, and was then roughly dragged to one of two sofa's sitting in front of a huge ornate stone fireplace.

'Sit there,' the white guy without a name said gruffly, his strong Essex accent making the two words sound like a threat.

Daisy and Aidan didn't need a second invitation, not that there was a first. Their lead-like legs didn't want to keep them standing very long.

Dismal failure tended to have that effect on a body.

No one had anything else to say. The two squad members wandered aimlessly around, trying to look like official guards, and Adde stood at the huge window, watching out for the Rolls to arrive. He didn't have to stand there long. The circular headlights threw momentary flashes of yellow light across the window, and then the purr of the engine died away.

Adde left the room, to let his mistress know her evening was not yet over. Daisy and Aidan heard the front door close, and the harsh Belgian tones of the lady of the chateau as the red stilettos clunked across the black and white tiles on the floor of the elegant main hall. The door to the sitting room was partly open, so her shrill annoyance was clear to hear.

'This had better be good, Henri. My evening was excruciatingly tiresome, and I only attended to keep up appearances. Now you tell me there are yet more things I must attend to... at this hour?'

'I think you will rather enjoy this matter, Mrs. deBruin.'

The vision in white fur strode impatiently through the door. But as soon as she saw who was sitting forlornly on her sofa, the smile on her face was at least equal to the sparkling diamonds adorning the tiara on her head.

'Oh, Henri,' she gushed. 'I think I *will* rather enjoy this matter.'

Chapter 39

The vision in black and white walked elegantly to the sofa, with all the grace and confidence of someone in total control of the moment.

'Well, Mr. and Mrs. Henderson, you cannot imagine how delighted I am that you took the trouble to visit me in my own home.'

'Oh, I think we can,' Aidan mumbled.

'I do hope Henri has extended our impeccable hospitality to you both.'

'Didn't even get a French fry,' said Daisy dejectedly.

Their host poured herself something alcoholic from the small bar in the corner of the room, tut-tutted a sickly grin to Adde. 'Henri, how remiss of you.' He just grinned back. 'No matter; where you are going, food and hospitality will be the least of your worries.'

'You won't get away with it, you evil plastic matriarch.'

She laughed disparagingly. 'Oh, I think I will, Daisy dear.'

'Third time lucky, maybe?'

'Oh... certainly, my dear. Henri failed to end your life twice, but he won't fail again, *will you, Henri?*'

His grin faded. 'No, ma'am. Your wish is my command.'

Daisy wanted to see how far she could push the plastic matriarch. 'I don't quite understand though, Carmella. Why were you so determined to kill me?'

She strode up to her guest, stood looking down on her like she couldn't believe the question had to be asked. '*Why?* My son explained to me you were the one who ruined his life. What is a mother supposed to do, other than take retribution?'

'Well, some would say he got what he deserved.'

186

'He was falsely accused of crimes he did not commit. Because of *you*, and your amateur-sleuthing interference.'

'You and I both know there was nothing false about it.'

She reacted badly to that, threw the remains of the Martini over Daisy's face, strode away angrily. 'And still, in the face of death, you disparage my precious son.'

'It's a dirty job, but someone's got to do it.'

'You walk a thin line, lying bitch.'

'Thin line? From what you have just said, there isn't a line to walk at all anymore. So I might as well shove my size sixes where it hurts.'

Carmella threw her head back, fighting the urge to do something she might regret. 'For sure you have an acid tongue, Daisy.'

'Famous for it. But it's all I have left, isn't it? The only thing you've got to do now is work out a way to get rid of us once and for all without implicating yourself.'

The fake smile was back. 'Ah, but you see my dear friend, I already have.'

'Oh. I see,' said Daisy, a little stunned by the confident words she didn't want to hear.

Carmella glanced at her diamond-encrusted watch. 'Henri, am I right in thinking the tide is just about to turn, and come in?'

He nodded. 'Yes, Mrs. deBruin. It has just turned. It is low tide now, but won't be for long.'

Aidan glanced nervously to Daisy. Adde seemed to know what he was talking about, and what Carmella was talking about too, ominously. Then she confirmed it.

'So you know what to do, Henri?'

'Yes ma'am. I know what you wish.'

'Then get these two out of my sight, and out of my life. Take your two... friends, and make it so.'

The three squad members started to move towards their captives. Aidan started to move towards the sports bag, but then Carmella called out. *'Wait!'*

The thugs stopped in their tracks, but Aidan had made it to the bag on the table. He turned round, shielding the phone screen from sight, as their host barked out a final instruction. 'Get their phones, drop them in sea water to kill them, so they can't call for help. Later on, after the deed is done, place them back in their pockets. Then no one will know any different. And do not disturb me with this matter again. I am sure you can handle things from here, Henri. There is plenty of rope in the boathouse. Now I am tired, so I will retire to my bed. Goodnight, and goodbye, my friends.'

She marched out of the room. Quickly Aidan turned off his phone, before anyone else saw Sarah's horrified face on the screen, and handed it to Adde. Denzil held out his hand to Daisy. She took it, defiant to the end.

'How kind of you to help me up, dear boy.'

He wrenched it away. 'You stupid old cow. I want your phone.'

'Oh really? Do forgive my dementure, Denzil. It creeps up on me, you know.'

He shook his head in a disgusted kind of way. *'Phone?'*

She handed it over. Then they were bundled out of the room, back onto the terrace, and along the wooden path to the quay heading. Adde headed to the boathouse, his two squad members leading their captives along the landing stage.

Daisy's mind was racing again, searching for possible escape routes. The gun was still in Adde's room, and the strong, young guys had their hands firmly in a vice-like grip behind their backs.

188

Escape routes were a bit thin on the ground, to say the least.

They stopped a few metres from the bow of the fishing cruiser, waiting for the thug they knew as Henri. Aidan looked over the side of the landing stage. The cruiser was just about floating on the low tide, but right below them it was mud.

He glanced to Daisy, and knew instantly she was thinking exactly the same as he was. The damp, gently sloping mud was exposed right then, but at high tide it would be anything but.

He threw his eyes to the dark sky. 'It would seem dear, that for the second time in a month our destiny lies in the hands of sea water.'

Chapter 40

Adde was back, coils of thick rope around his shoulders. He pointed to an access ladder a few metres away. 'Down there,' he said curtly. 'You aren't so decrepit you can't use a ladder, I take it?'

'Your scintillating wit will be the death of me, Adde.'

He showed her the Wallace and Gromit grin again. 'Funny thing, I don't need any wit to help with your death, Daisy.'

Suddenly, Aidan made a last-ditch move, broke free of Denzil's grip and lashed out backwards. He caught the thug in the face. He cried out, lunged back at him. So did the other two. He didn't stand a chance. One of them punched him in the stomach. Daisy cried out, knowing his brave last-chance-saloon move was futile.

'Ok... just leave him be. We'll do as you say.'

'At least one of you's got some sense.'

Aidan straightened up, wheezing a little. He smiled to Daisy, letting her know he was unharmed. But the smile had an air of desolate acceptance about it. He knew as well as she did there was no escape.

One by one they descended the short ladder to the muddy but firm ground eight feet below. They were bustled to the support posts of the landing stage, ordered to sit.

'You want me to get a soggy butt?' said Daisy.

Denzil took a length of rope from Adde's shoulder. 'Believe me lady, a soggy butt will seem like a distant memory soon.'

The white guy who still didn't have a name was busy tying Aidan to the next post. 'Can you have memories when you're dead?' he asked.

190

'Dunno. Ain't never got the chance to find out.'

The three thugs laughed at their own joke. Then Adde was there, pulling their legs out flat, and tying more rope around their middles, just to make sure. And then he took great delight in explaining what was to happen next, even though they'd already worked it out.

'So guys, you see that green line just above your heads?'

Daisy glanced up to the line of weed five inches above her head. She'd already spotted it, but she played his game anyway. 'I take it that's how far up high tide gets? Once it's drowned us, as the tide recedes you'll cut our bodies free, put the phones back in our pockets, and then let the outgoing tide take us into the estuary. So when they find us, there are no signs of anything other than accidental drowning, and you and your mistress can't be implicated.'

He grinned. 'See, you're not so demented after all. Except for your brainless antics earlier.'

'They weren't brainless, Adde. If you had kids, you'd know how they determine your actions.'

'Aw Daisy... and now you'll never know what happened to Celia, will you?'

She lowered her head, and he saw a tear roll down her cheek. And then he had a moment of sympathy. 'She meant a lot, I guess?'

She almost whispered the words, the sheer emotion of finality making it impossible to speak any louder. 'Since you took her, we've spent over three years trying to find out what happened to our daughter. Trying to find closure, one way or another. You have any idea how important that is? At least I'll go to my grave knowing you didn't kill her.'

'Aw, geez, lady. Don't you get me tearing up now.'

'Sorry.'

He sighed. 'Look... it ain't gonna matter none now, but you've just sent me all soft. Maybe you should bow out knowing, if it makes that much difference to you. I ain't got no idea exactly where she is now, but she was sold to a high-ranking government official in Uganda.'

'Not *Museveni*?'

'What, that ancient pensioner? Ain't even sure he can still get it up. Nah, he was younger.'

'Not that it makes any difference now, but do you have a name?'

He stood up. 'You's right. It don't matter now. But I don't have a name anyway. It wasn't the done thing in that industry, and transactions were all cash. That's all I know, for what good it does you now.'

'Actually, it helps a lot. Thank you, Adde.'

He tramped away, calling back as he climbed the ladder to the landing stage where his squad was waiting. 'And by the way, I didn't get to have my way with her. I just said that to piss you off. I tried to, but she fought like hell so I gave it up as a shit job.'

'Good for her,' whispered Aidan, so Adde couldn't hear.

'Yeah, good for her,' echoed Daisy.

They heard the clunk of footsteps on the landing stage above their heads as the three thugs headed to the fishing cruiser. Then the sweet tones of Denzil's voice wafted across the crisp night air.

'Hey, boss... those Macydee's cokes are still in your room. You wanna fetch them so we can finish them while we fish?'

Adde seemed to think it was a good idea. 'Sure. There's beers on the boat, but we might as well finish the cokes first, seeing as you paid for them! I'll get 'em, you two rig up the rods. We can't cruise anywhere, given the... situation, but we can fish off the rear well.'

Then they heard more footsteps above them, as Adde went to fetch the drinks. Daisy glanced to Aidan, tied firmly to the next post four feet from her. 'Looks like we'll have company while we drown, dear.'

He nodded his head. 'We're not drowned yet, Flower.'

'No, but if the cavalry don't get here soon, we will be. I was thinking...'

'I know. The irony isn't lost on me. Yet again we're at the mercy of seawater, except this time it's not us dropping down *into* the water, it's the water rising up to meet us.'

She let out a mirthless chuckle. 'Yet again you've hit the nail on the head, dear. But on the subject of comparisons, I was actually thinking something else.'

'What's that?'

She looked him straight in his sad eyes, even though in the dark shadows where the deck lights didn't shine, she could hardly see them. 'I was thinking that at least the last time we were facing death by ocean, we were able to do it in each other's arms. This time we're tied up four feet apart, and I can't even hold your hand as we perish.'

Chapter 41

It was a beautiful night in Belgium. A bright half-moon cast a little light across the incoming tide, the wind was virtually nonexistent, and the water that covered their legs was nowhere near as cold as it could have been.

Occasionally container ships would pass across their limited viewpoint, a mile or so in the distance. Their blazing lights reflected serenely off the calm water, their crews completely unaware two people were close to losing their lives just a mile away.

Even if someone was peering through binoculars, all they would have seen were three men fishing off the stern of a boat tied to a landing stage, its back end facing into the estuary. The two people about to be murdered were well hidden, twenty feet the other side of its bow, and in almost complete darkness.

No one would ever see them from the water.

'The tide comes in quite quickly,' said Aidan, letting out a slight shiver.

'Did you have to say that?'

'Sorry, dear. It's because the slope of the ground here is shallow. Now the sea has covered the mud, it will appear to go slower.'

'Dip, sometimes your galactic-sized brain isn't that encouraging.'

'Sorry, dear.'

Daisy glanced down to the water, gently lapping against her lower stomach. 'Where the hell are Sarah and Burrows?'

'Well I could offer a thought or two, but you've virtually told me to shut up.'

'Ok, so now I'm telling you to say something.'

'Make your mind up.'

'Dear, we're about to drown... again... please stop being so pedantic.'

'What I was going to say is not really that encouraging.'

'Just say it, for god's sake.'

'They're coming via the USAF. We don't know what time that flight left, but even when they get to Belgium it's almost certain they'll land at the USAF base near Brussels, which is forty miles from here.'

'Now I wish you weren't so brainy.'

'They might have persuaded the Belgian police to mobilise themselves, but...'

'There always has to be a *but*.'

'Yes, and the but is Carmella clearly has some high-ranking officials in her pocket, so even if they do raid the place, all they'll find is her asleep in bed.'

Daisy shook her head despondently. 'And the video call to Sarah was killed before she knew how they were going to do us in.'

'Which means a half-hearted police raid won't even bother with what's lying at the bottom of her garden, hidden from sight. I told you it wasn't exactly encouraging.'

'No dear, but even though your immense brain is working out nothing but depressing equations, for some inexplicable reason I still love you.'

They could hear the merry sounds of the three men happily fishing away from the other end of the boat. It didn't seem to please Daisy.

'How the hell can they just sit there enjoying a relaxing night's fishing, when two old codgers are about to drown?'

There was a hint of desperation mixed in with the anger, but there wasn't much Aidan could say to make it better. 'I guess some people are just missing a conscience.'

'Yeah, and we just happened along to prove it to them.'

Then it seemed one of them did have a conscience after all. At the bow fifteen feet away, the white guy was suddenly standing looking down on them, the coke cup still in his hand. He didn't look as full of the joys of spring as the rest of his squad.

'Still not dead then?' he said.

'Don't worry, we'll be there soon,' Daisy retorted.

'Look...' He sat down on the forward cabin roof. 'For what it's worth, I ain't happy about this. Killing old folks ain't my bag.'

'Then come and untie us,' said Aidan, more in hope than expectation.

'Sorry. Outvoted there. My squad leader, he's got too much to lose if you live.'

'We've got too much to lose if we die.'

He glanced round to the stern of the boat, looked like he was in two minds. For a fleeting moment Daisy felt a waft of hope flood through her heart. But then it was dashed, stone dead.

'Can't do it. Sorry. But I can't stick around either, watching this shit happen. I'm calling it a night.'

He stood up, and it looked like the conversation was over. Daisy pleaded one last time. '*Please,* do the decent thing. I'll be your friend forever... and then you won't be an accessory to murder. I'll put in a good word.'

Again he hesitated, like he didn't know what to do. Then he shook his head. 'Nah. More than my life's worth.'

'And what is our life worth?'

He started to walk away. 'Not enough. I'm off.'

'Hey... if you're not going to help, at least give me a drink? I'm dying of thirst here.'

He grinned, but didn't stop walking away. Then he threw the polystyrene cup to her. 'Here, seeing as you still got your sense of humour.'

He was gone. They heard a few words spoken between the thugs, and then the clunk of footsteps over their heads. Whoever the reluctant thug was, he was totally gone.

The McDonald's cup had landed just short of Daisy. As the incoming tide drifted it over her legs, she lifted her knees out of the water and trapped it between them. She leant her head forward as far as it would go, sucked in the last dregs of coke through the fat straw.

'Dear, I'm sorry. There was only a smidgen left. It's empty now. I was going to share, but there wasn't enough.'

'It's ok, Flower. If the cavalry doesn't arrive in the next hour or so, being thirsty will be the least of my problems.'

'Please don't say that.'

'We've got to face up to harsh facts, dear. Our heads are only a foot above the water now.'

Then, as he looked sadly at his wife, a sudden thought occurred to him. He glanced up to the weed line, just a few inches above their heads. When he spoke again, his voice held a new kind of urgency.

'Dear, whatever you do, don't let go of that cup.'

Chapter 42

Daisy looked at him like he already had water on the brain. 'Dear, it's empty, no use to either of us.'

'*I said don't let it go.* It is useful, for one of us anyway.'

'I don't understand.'

'When... if the water level gets above your head, you can use that thick straw as a breathing pipe. For a while longer anyway.'

She looked at him, but didn't let go of the polystyrene cup between her legs. Then she shook her head. 'And what about you, you dipstick? You suddenly sprouted gills?'

'Funny girl.' Daisy saw his head lower, heard his softly-spoken words. 'If just one of us survives dear, then she can go on to find Celia. Adde told us where he sold her, remember? She might not be in Uganda anymore, but it's a hell of a stronger starting point than we've ever had before.'

His voice choked a little, he had to clear his throat. Daisy wasn't sure if it was desolate emotion, or the chill of the water. 'To make use of that information, one of us has to go on. And you're better equipped than me to act on it, let's face it.'

'Not without you I'm not, Dip.' Daisy felt a tear roll down her cheek, but there was no way to wipe it away.

'*Yes, you are.* If it comes to it, that's the way it has to be.'

'No! If I let this cup go, it'll drift to you, so you don't have a choice in the matter anyway.'

'Daisy! Are you blackmailing me?'

'If I have to, yes.'

'Well it won't work. If I refuse to catch it, then we'll both drown.'

'Your stubborn streak is mortally frustrating me now.'

'*Mine?*'

'Yes, yours.' Another tear made its way down her face. 'So prepare for launch of polystyrene cup.'

'Don't you dare, you stupid cow. Just listen to someone else, for once in your life.'

'Dip...'

He lifted his eyes to the starry sky, shook his head against the post, and then closed his eyes to ward off the tears. 'Are you listening to us, arguing about which one of us is going to *live*?'

'Well, it's not an argument we've had before.'

He let out a mirthless, choky kind of laugh. 'And not one we'll ever have again, I think.'

'You're not wrong there.'

He glanced over to her, saw her body shaking in the water. 'Dear, I love you. And all I want to do now is hold you close, but I can't. So all I can say to make my case is that there's more at stake than an old man's life. Our daughter's future is on the line, and if we're both dead, neither of us can be there to change that for her.'

Daisy let out a sob she'd tried so hard to hold in. 'You're killing me with your words, you lovely, stupid man.'

He tried to ignore the pain of seeing the woman he loved in anguish. 'So do we have a deal? he whispered.

'It's not going to come to that,' she whispered back, more in vain hope than because she believed it.

'And when... if it does, *do we have a deal*?' he said, a little louder.

'You're asking me to sign your death warrant.'

'That's part of the deal. It's about our daughter, as you keep telling me.'

'You drive a hard bargain, you selfless bastard.'

'Deal?'
'Deal.'

Things grew a little quieter. The two thugs still on the boat seemed to tire of fishing, but there were no sounds of footsteps on the wooden deck above their heads. It seemed like they'd retreated to the cabin, likely to get merry on cans of beer while they waited for the tide to do its deadly work.

There was no sound of muffled voices anymore. There was no sound of anything. As midnight came and went, even the container ships seemed to stop passing by. Nothing moved, except the tide, relentlessly rising, with no King Canute suddenly appearing to stem its inevitable progress.

Daisy was still holding the precious cup between her knees, but it had become a little easier. The seawater may have been warm for the time of year, but once she'd been in it for several hours on a September night, it felt colder than she would have liked.

But it had one bonus. Keeping her knees around the cup wasn't something she had to concentrate on doing anymore. Her body had set under the water, and the cup with its life-saving straw was staying where it was without any effort on her part.

The water was up to her chin. More than she'd ever done, she longed to reach out a hand to wrap around Aidan's, but even that last, desperate comfort was denied her. Both their hands were tied securely at the back of their personal posts, and as she'd cried tears of desolation, she knew the man she loved was going to be ripped from her life without even the consolation of a final touch.

She didn't want to live without him, but she couldn't argue with his logic. The stakes were about more than just them, more than just Aidan. Adde had experienced a moment of compassion, and let slip where their daughter was, believing neither of them would survive to tell the tale.

There was still no guarantee either of them would survive. Living was by no means a certainty. But the cavalry would come, eventually. And maybe the fat McDonald's straw would give one of them the means to breathe long enough to be rescued.

One of them.

Daisy shuddered again, but this time it was nothing to do with the cold. She felt the tears try to come once more, but a while back she'd told herself to be strong for the man she loved. It was important to her that when he looked at her for the last time, he saw a smile on her face.

She turned her head to glance to him. 'I'm holding your hand, Dip. Here, in my heart. Can you feel it?'

He lifted his head a little, spat away the seawater that was lapping around his lips, and smiled back. 'Of course I can feel it. And I am squeezing it tight, and never letting go. Can you feel that?'

She tried to nod, but it wasn't the best idea. Struggling to hold her emotions together, the water was flowing into her open mouth at the lowest part of the nod. She lifted her head, and said words instead.

'You are crushing my hand in your iron grip. So don't ever let go. Not ever.'

'I promise,' he whispered.

'I love you.'

'I love you too.'

Daisy closed her eyes to force away the mistiness. It would very soon be time to use her lips to pull the straw

201

from its cup, and say a final goodbye to the man she loved as she watched him drown.

It was the last sight on Earth she wanted to witness, but she couldn't not watch. For Aidan's sake, so he knew she was there beside him until the very last second of his life.

Then, as her vision cleared, she saw something else. At any other time, it wasn't anything out of the ordinary.

But right then, right there, it was the most beautiful sight in the universe.

Chapter 43

'*Dip...*' Daisy stage-whispered. '*Look.*'

He turned his head to follow her gaze, blinked away his tears. '*Oh my god,*' he spluttered.

There, drifting towards them on the incoming tide, was the last sight either of them had expected to see. Just clearing the bow of the boat, highlighted by the swathes of light from the deck lamps, two white McDonald coke cups were heading their way.

And they both still had their straws.

Daisy spat the seawater out of her mouth, lifted her head as high as it would go. 'Can you move, catch one of them?'

Aidan groaned out the words weakly. '*I think so...*'

'Use the knees on those long legs of yours... I can't move.'

'Daisy, you need to grab your straw now. The water's getting too high.'

She did as he said, made a super-human effort and managed to lift her legs so the cup between her knees was as close to her head as she could get it. It was still just beneath the surface, so she sucked in a deep breath and dropped her head into the water.

One second later her face was above the water again, the straw firmly between her lips. She had her breathing pipe, but talking then was impossible. She couldn't utter another single word of encouragement to Aidan.

He could still talk. 'Very soon you'll be under the water. Tip your head back as far as it will go, and the straw will point as far up as it can. Let's just pray it will be far enough. Good luck, darling.'

She nodded furiously, all she could do to let him know she understood. They both watched as the two polystyrene cups floated ever nearer. Daisy thought a weird kind of thank you to their two captives, eternally grateful they'd discarded their rubbish over the side of their boat rather than bother with a waste bin.

Then her heart sank. Both of the cups were passing by too far away. Even Aidan's long legs would never reach them.

He cried out, *'No...'*

She closed her eyes, realising the last hope the man she loved would survive was gone. The two cups floated past him, just a couple of feet away from being caught. It looked like his last chance had floated away on the tide.

But then something happened that neither of them could have foreseen.

Seawater behaves in strange ways when it is pushed by the tide into an enclosed space. And where they were imprisoned *was* an enclosed space. The narrow inlet had been cut into the grounds, just wide enough for the landing stage and twenty feet of water either side of it, to allow boats to moor.

The rectangular, three-sided creek was only as long as the landing stage itself. As the tide came in, it reached a dead-end. But seawater was never still, and it had to move somewhere. As Daisy and Aidan watched in disbelief, the two cups reached the end of the inlet, and began to head back towards them.

Caught in a gentle arcing swirl, this time they were closer. Daisy heard Aidan whisper a determined groan to psyche himself up, and as one of the cups drifted back by him, lifted his legs and caught it. The cup and his legs disappeared below the surface, the effort of catching the cup as much as his stiff legs could manage.

'Daisy cried out an *'Mmm'* of encouragement, nodding her head furiously again to help him find the strength he needed.

'I'm getting there, dear,' he whispered hoarsely.

He lifted his legs towards his head, probably the last time he would be able to make such a move, and his head disappeared below the surface, just as Daisy's had done.

Then it was back, the straw between his lips.

Daisy's heart sang. It was a moment she would remember for the rest of her life... however long that was.

Neither of them could speak anymore. It didn't matter. Now both of them had a chance of survival, and suddenly the telepathic link they'd forged over the years was more important than ever.

As they both tipped their heads back and pointed their straws into the air, and the water lapped around their faces, Daisy closed her eyes. Maybe they couldn't speak; couldn't even see each other anymore. But she could feel his love and encouragement, flowing into her, making her stronger.

And she just knew it was exactly the same for him.

Chapter 44

Officer Sarah Lowry and her boss were driven up to the gates of the chateau, in the back of a Belgian police car Burrows had rather forcibly insisted pick them up from the air base.

The Belgian chief of police hadn't exactly been pleased he'd been wrenched from the bed he'd just climbed into after the ambassador's ball, but when he'd been told they had proof of Carmella deBruin's involvement in murder, he knew he had no choice but to act.

As they drove past the police car parked just inside the entrance gates, Sarah and Burrows knew he *had* taken action.

The forecourt lights were blazing away, illuminating the small crowd standing outside the front entrance. Most of them seemed to be staff members, looking extremely bemused, and guarded by a few policemen with weapons. Two of the crowd weren't staff. The lady of the chateau looked furious, pacing up and down in her black silk nightgown covered by a pure white robe. The red stilettos were on her feet, adding to the slightly-comical sight. Clearly she didn't appreciate having her beauty-sleep disturbed.

As Sarah and Burrows stepped from the car, someone else didn't look too pleased either. Pierre Richelau marched up to them, an angry expression on his face. 'This had better be good, Inspecteur. I have had to drag a fine upstanding citizen of Belgium from her bed... and I have a golf match in the morning. This is acutely embarrassing, especially as my men have found nothing.'

'Nothing?'

'Nothing, so far. We are just completing the search of the house and the servant's quarters, but so far there is nothing to suggest any wrongdoing. I hope you have a reasonable explanation.'

Carmella thundered up to them. '*You again?* Pierre, perhaps you will put an end to this farce, so I can return to my bed. And these incompetent British police officers can go back to their pitiful little country where they belong.'

Pierre looked acutely embarrassed. It didn't get any better for him when one of his men appeared, and told him they had completed the search and found nothing. He turned to the spitting, fuming lady of the chateau and lifted his hands from his sides. 'Carmella...'

'Excuse me,' Sarah butted in. 'We told you we had proof.' She pulled the phone from her pocket, fiddled with a few buttons, and held it out so the two of them could watch the screen. The picture was less than clear, blurred by the netting of the drinks pocket, but it was still sharp enough to make out who was present. The voices however, were as clear as day.

'I do hope Henri has extended our impeccable hospitality to you both.'

'Didn't even get a French fry.'

'Henri, how remiss of you. No matter; where you are going, food and hospitality will be the least of your worries.'

'You won't get away with it, you evil plastic matriarch.'

'Oh, I think I will, Daisy dear.'

'Third time lucky, maybe?'

'Oh... certainly, my dear. Henri failed to end your life twice, but he won't fail again, will you, Henri?'

'No, ma'am. Your wish is my command.'

'I don't quite understand though, Carmella. Why were you so determined to kill me?'

207

'Why? My son explained to me you were the one who ruined his life. What is a mother supposed to do, other than take retribution?'

'Well, some would say he got what he deserved.'

'He was falsely accused of crimes he did not commit. Because of you, and your amateur-sleuthing interference.'

'You and I both know there was nothing false about it.'

'And still, in the face of death, you disparage my precious son.'

'It's a dirty job, but someone's got to do it.'

'You walk a thin line, lying bitch.'

'Thin line? From what you have just said, there isn't a line to walk at all anymore. So I might as well shove my size sixes where it hurts.'

'For sure you have an acid tongue, Daisy.'

'Famous for it. But it's all I have left, isn't it? The only thing you've got to do now is work out a way to get rid of us once and for all without implicating yourself.'

'Ah, but you see my dear friend, I already have...'

As she listened to the words, Carmella's face turned from disparaging fury to a completely different kind of fury. She gasped out the words. *How... give me that phone...'*

She lunged at Sarah, but the chief of police was already on the move, grabbing her flailing arms, and pinning them behind her back. 'Mrs. deBruin, I am sorry, but...'

Sarah had taken a step back, but then felt a triumphant smile spread across her face. She moved closer to the shocked Carmella, held out the phone. 'Here... take it. Stamp your stilettos furiously on it if you want. I've already emailed the video to myself... just in case.'

The vision in black and white screamed out her frustration, but the chief of police who had once been in her pocket had already handed her to one of his men, who was bundling her, still making empty threats, into one of the police cars.

Sarah had more important things on her mind. She looked around the still-bemused faces of the staff. None of them were Adde Wambua. 'Where is Ad... Henri?' she cried out.

'I am sorry, he is not here. Perhaps he saw us arriving, and escaped.'

'And you have not found our two friends?'

Pierre shook his head. 'There is no sign...'

'*No...* you're not looking hard enough...'

She ran to the corner of the house, closely followed by Burrows and Richelau. As she walked quickly to the rear garden, her thoughts were racing. The thugs had fled, but somehow she knew Daisy and Aidan were still there. She reached the rear terrace, stopped and looked around. Desperate hands flew to her head as her eyes panned the rear grounds.

What did Carmella say on the video? *'Get their phones, drop them in sea water to kill them, so they can't call for help. Later on, after the deed is done, place them back in their pockets. Then no one will know any different. There is plenty of rope in the boathouse...*

She glanced to Burrows, her eyes wide with fear. 'They're down there, somewhere around the landing stage.'

'How...' he started to say.

The chief of police shook his head. 'We have already looked there. There is nothing but the fishing cruiser, and that is empty.'

Sarah started to run towards the landing stage she'd seen once before. 'Then you are the incompetent ones,

209

Inspector. They're there somewhere... *I just hope we're not too late...'*

Chapter 45

They ran onto the landing stage. It looked empty. just as Richelau said. The fishing cruiser sat at the end of the stage, in darkness. Sarah panned her eyes around. It was high tide, the deck lights were still on, but she knew from previous stowaway experience they were rarely switched off.

'Where are they?' she cried, throwing a hand to her head again.

Ropes. Carmella had said something about ropes.

'Anyone got a torch?' she almost screamed.

Pierre Richelau handed her the one clipped to his belt. It wasn't exactly powerful, but as she panned it across the surface of the water just below them, she saw something.

Then her heart sank. It was just two old McDonald's polystyrene cups that someone had discarded, floated in by the tide, and now on their way out again.

She threw a panic-stricken glance to her boss, but then in the silence of the night, she heard something. A muffled, faint voice, that sounded for all the world like someone was making a demented kind of *'mmm'* sound through a pipe.

She panned the torch downwards again, closer to the stage. And then she saw them. Two tiny pipes were sticking through the surface, and one of them was waggling furiously.

'Oh my god...'

She didn't hesitate. Screaming at the chief of police to call an ambulance and find thermal blankets, she jumped straight into the water.

She knew it couldn't be that deep, not just there. Even with her petite frame, the water was only just up to her chin. As she reached down into the murky water and her hands wrapped around one of her friends, she heard a splash behind her. Burrows was there to.

'Knife... I need a knife. They're tied up...'

He was beside her, handing her a pocket knife. Like a crazed ninja she hacked away at the ropes. Then there was another splash behind her, as a Belgian officer joined them. He had a knife too, and began sawing at Aidan's ropes.

Hands were free, flailing above the water. A minute later, bodies were free too. Another officer jumped in, and together they wrenched Daisy and Aidan clear of the water. Sarah almost fell into Daisy, wrapped supportive arms around her as she helped her stand against the supporting post she'd been tied to a minute earlier.

She gasped and wheezed, as Sarah's hands brushed the sodden hair from her face. Cloudy, disbelieving eyes locked into the girl who had just saved her. Still Daisy coughed, as her lungs got used to the freedom of unlimited fresh air. Her first words were clear enough though.

'You took your time.'

Sarah grinned, as they threw relieved arms around each other.

The men virtually carried Daisy and Aidan from the water, up the short ladder and onto the deck, just as two paramedics ran up, and wrapped them in silver thermal blankets. Daisy reached out a hand to Aidan, sitting on his butt looking a little worse for wear.

'There you go, see Dip? Ronald McDonald to the rescue! And you two, of course.' She threw a grateful glance to Sarah and Burrows.

Aidan slipped off his oxygen mask, shook his head at his wife, who was grinning to him through the blanket draped like a hooded cloak around her head. Her eyes were soaking wet, and he couldn't tell if it was seawater or tears, but he knew her well enough to know which it was. 'Dear, I would say you'll be the death of me, but that doesn't seem quite appropriate right now.'

Burrows put a hand on Daisy's shoulder. 'You two must be hypothermic. Let's get you to the hospital, have you checked out. And yes, you'll be the death of me, for sure!'

Daisy nodded, tried to stand up but her legs wouldn't work. One of the paramedics said they'd fetch stretchers, but Daisy refused. With the help of two people, she got to her feet. Aidan did the same, but looked very unsteady.

But they both looked happy, and somewhat surprised, to be alive.

Then something happened that no one expected. Every one of the eight people on the landing stage were facing the house, all of their attentions taken up with Daisy and Aidan's rescue and recovery.

No one saw there was suddenly a ninth person on the landing stage. Knowing they were all concentrating on the two elderly people who had cheated death by minutes, Adde Wambua had seized his moment.

Denzil's shadowy figure had crept onto the deck, slipped the mooring ropes from the posts and jumped back aboard. As the tide which had just started to run back out helped the boat to drift clear of the landing stage and beyond reach, Adde fired up the engines.

No one on the landing stage even knew the two of them were hiding on board the fishing cruiser. All their attention taken up with the rescue, nobody had even realised the boat was drifting free.

But as the sound of its twin engines wafted their unmistakable noise across the still, dark water, and eight

213

faces turned to look at the disappearing boat in horror, each one knew for sure the real murderers were about to get away.

And there wasn't a thing they could do about it.

Chapter 46

Then something else happened. Something they *really* hadn't expected.

As Daisy, Sarah and Burrows ran to the end of the deck, one of them stumbling along on useless legs, kept upright by the other two, another boat appeared out of the darkness.

This one was a lot smaller, and didn't have a cabin. It was all varnished wood which reflected the deck lights back as it cruised up to the end of the landing stage, piloted by a man with a cheery, moustached face.

'*Felix!*' cried a shocked Daisy.

'Seriously?' said an even more shocked Sarah.

'Good evening, my friends,' called Felix. 'I decided to borrow a boat, knowing it was a possibility someone might try to escape by water.'

'You lovely man,' coughed Daisy.

'Do you want me to follow them?'

'Course we do,' said Sarah. 'But I'm coming too.'

'So am I,' growled Daisy.'

'Daisy? You're in no fit...'

'I can sit in a boat, can't I?'

Burrows shook his head, like he'd already expected his pain-in-the-neck to be a pain in the neck. 'Daisy, we can call the coastguard. They'll pick them up.'

She was already almost falling into the launch, with Sarah's help, who knew better than to argue. 'Call them anyway, sir. But this coastline is full of little bays and inlets... trust me, I know. By the time the coastguard gets here they'll be landed somewhere, and escape on foot.'

He threw his hands in the air, but then pulled his phone out anyway. Felix grinned, and opened the throttle. The fast launch sped away, and disappeared into the darkness.

'Just like old times, yes my friend?'

Daisy, already shivering under the blanket, her wet clothes not helping to make her any warmer, smiled her agreement. 'Don't suppose you've got any dry clothes hidden somewhere?'

'Sadly not, Daisy dear. But this chase should be over soon.'

The white fishing cruiser was a quarter of a mile in front of them. The launch was fast, but not fast enough. They were gaining on the cruiser, but only just. They were three hundred yards behind it when it turned to the left and headed for the coastline just a half mile away. Daisy watched it in dismay.

'Felix, in about three minutes they'll be on dry land. We've got to stop them. Forget dry clothes, you got a gun anywhere on board?'

He handed her his luger. Sarah looked at it in horror. 'Daisy, you can't shoot them!'

'I'm not going to shoot *them*. Just the boat, stop them cruising until the coastguard gets here.'

'Isn't there another way?'

A bullet whizzed past them, hitting the water twenty feet away. Denzil was standing on the rear deck, doing all he could to make sure they escaped.

'Got your answer now?' Daisy grinned, lifting the gun ready to fire back.

She fired, but the bullet was way off the mark. Several hours of being marinated in seawater meant every bit of her was shaking itself to bits.

'Bugger.'

'Oh, give me the gun,' said Sarah, grabbing it from Daisy's shaking hands. 'You couldn't even hit me right now.'

'Shoot the tyres,' said Daisy, frustrated she didn't stand a chance of doing it herself.

'What?'

'It's got outdrives... they're just above the surface. Knock them out and the engines are useless.'

Sarah aimed the gun at the two protruding outdrives on the stern of the boat. Aiming wasn't easy from a moving boat. She fired off three shots. Two of them missed, but one hit the port outdrive. There was a sound like grating gears, and then it looked like it stopped working. The cruiser slowed a little, but still had one working drive to help it limp to shore.

Another bullet spat into the water, a little closer this time. Denzil was still in the stern well, and taking aim again. Felix slowed the launch to match the cruisers reduced speed, reluctant to get any closer. Daisy put a hand on Sarah's waist. 'Good girl. Now see if you can knobble the starboard drive, then we can get to a safe distance and let the coastguard deal with them.'

'It's not easy, Daisy. Hitting a moving target from a moving target, I mean.'

'Do your best.'

Sarah fired again, another three shots. And then the third thing happened none of them expected.

The cruiser exploded in a ball of flames.

Felix throttled back the launch, stood up in his seat staring at the flaming wreckage in disbelief. *'Petrol-driven?* You've got to be kidding me.'

217

Sarah slumped down in the seat, tears in her eyes. '*I killed them, Daisy,*' she whispered.

She pulled the distraught girl close. 'Hey, you weren't to know. And they were firing on us. You had every right to fire back.'

Felix sat down, put a hand on Sarah's shoulder. 'Listen, brave girl. Almost every boat in these parts is diesel-powered. But that looked like an American fishing cruiser. Over there, petrol marine engines are still common. The deBruin's must have imported it, petrol engines and all.'

Sarah sniffed back the tears. 'You're both right, but it doesn't make it much easier. Can we see if there are any survivors?'

Felix shook his head but opened the throttle anyway, and they cruised in a big circle around the wreckage. What was left of the hull had sunk, leaving a tragic circle of nothing but flaming flotsam. The fuel tanks must have been almost full, and there was likely a propane cylinder or two aboard too, which hadn't helped.

Then they heard the beating blades of a helicopter, and a minute later the chopper flew into view, spotted them and hovered to check they were ok.

Felix waved to say they were, and then opened the throttle wider and turned the launch back towards the landing stage.

Daisy lifted Sarah's chin from her chest. 'Hey, my dear friend. I'm starting to lose track of the number of times you've saved my life. Perhaps Adde Wambua and his second in command didn't deserve to lose theirs, but they did try and kill me, several times. So maybe something up there is telling me it's not my time yet, and you're the angel making sure of that.'

Sarah buried her head in Daisy's shoulder. 'It's a dirty job, but someone's got to do it.'

Chapter 47

Daisy watched DCI Burrows' eyes as he read the statement he'd asked her and Aidan to compile. Sitting on the opposite side of the desk in his office, she waited patiently for him to finish.

He dropped it back on the desk, and shook his head in the despairing way she'd got used to seeing. 'You really are a pain in my butt, Daisy Morrow.'

'I know, Inspector. But just think what life would be like without us in it.'

'Oh trust me, I often do. But somehow you seem to come out of it smelling of roses each time. Or daisies maybe.'

Aidan, sitting next to Daisy, laughed. 'Just be grateful, Inspector. I have to smell the daisies every day!'

Daisy scowled at him, but there was a smile on her face. 'So what's the upshot of it all?'

Burrows had a hint of a smile on his craggy face. 'Well, Adde Wambua can't be prosecuted because he's not here anymore. Some would say he got his just desserts.'

'That includes Aidan and me.'

'I'm sure it does. But thanks to you two and Officer Lowry acting in an *unofficial* capacity, Belgian police are going to bring Carmella deBruin to justice. The videos you secretly made aren't strictly-speaking admissible in court, but combined with the dried blood evidence you *finally* admitted to finding, there isn't much doubt she will go away for a very long time.'

'Sarah only kept it from you because I begged her to, Inspector. I realise she, um... bent protocol a bit, but I hope you can see the greater good. Will she be punished at all?'

220

He stood up, walked to the window and stood looking out with his hands in his pockets. 'I *should* punish her. But on the other hand, her work and her initiative resulted in bringing two criminals to justice. So am I biting off the hand that feeds me, Daisy?'

'If you punish her, you will be, Inspector.'

He turned back into the room. 'I had a feeling you were going to say that.'

'Of course we were,' said Aidan. 'She's the best thing that's ever happened to you.'

He sat down again, and smiled. 'I'll take that with a pinch of hot curry sauce, Aidan.'

Daisy had something else on her mind. 'It's been three days now, Inspector, and she's still beating herself up about what happened at the end. Even though she only did what she had to, and because I had the shakes and couldn't. I think she needs a little time to recover.'

His eyes clouded over. 'Me too. She's still a rookie cop, and things like that can affect an inexperienced officer for years... sometimes for ever. I suppose you have a suggestion?'

'As it happens...'

'Why did I get the feeling you were going to say that?'

'She needs a break, time to pull herself back together. And she saved our lives when even we thought no one would. We'd like to take Sarah and ourselves away for a couple of weeks... a little holiday to say thank you and fix her back up.'

He nodded like he understood. 'Ok. When?'

'As soon as we can book the flights. In the next few days for sure.'

'So be it. I'll authorise the time off, on medical grounds. I'll leave it to you to do the rest.'

Daisy and Aidan walked through the squad room on their way out, paused at Sarah's desk. 'We're going to do a little shopping in the city, and then grab some lunch. You want to join us?'

'I'll have to see if it's okay with Burrows.'

Daisy put a hand on her shoulder. 'It'll be fine, trust me. Call you when we're ready to eat.'

They spent an hour shopping in the Kings Lynn mall, and then Aidan was looking like he'd had enough. In truth, Daisy felt the same. It had only been three days since their ordeal by seawater, and Sarah wasn't the only one who needed recovery time.

The trip to the city had really only been made for one reason. The statement Daisy and Aidan had written had been worded in such a way to make sure Sarah couldn't be blamed for anything. Burrows hadn't been on their back about getting it to him, it could just as easily have been posted in.

Taking it to him in person had been an excuse to make sure he gave Sarah time off. That was important to Daisy and Aidan, and there was more than one reason for that too.

Sarah grinned as she walked into the restaurant and found the two of them waiting for her at a red plastic table. 'I thought this would be the last place you'd want to be!'

'Hey, I'm taking Aidan here for our anniversary next time,' Daisy grinned.

He laughed, but there was a genuine sense of relief in it. 'Let's face it, if it hadn't been for McDonald's fat straws, we wouldn't be here now!'

Sarah couldn't help a shudder racking her body. 'Tell me about it.'

Daisy stood up quickly. 'Ok, enough of that. Let's go and get food.'

She slipped an arm into Sarah's, and marched her to the counter. Five minutes later they were back with a tray full of burgers and fries.

Sarah unwrapped her Big Tasty. 'So, how did it go with the boss?'

'Fine. He's fully exonerated you of any criminal proceedings,' Daisy grinned.

'I suppose that's something,' Sarah said, looking less than pleased.

'And he thinks you should take time off to recover.'

'Oh... I'm fine. I'm a survivor.'

'So are we, apparently. But you're not fine. Trust me, I know.'

'Maybe you'll tell me how you know one day.'

'One day, dear. But right now, it's all arranged.'

'What is?'

'Your time off.'

Sarah narrowed her eyes. 'Daisy, what did you do?'

'Nothing... well, we just suggested we all go away on a little holiday, to say thank you to you for us actually being able to have one.'

'And Burrows said yes?'

'Of course. He's not such a bad old stick really.'

'Wow... I suppose I could do with a break. So where are we going?'

'Africa!' Daisy and Aidan said together.

'How did I know you were going to say that?'

'Don't you start.'

223

The burgers were eaten, and Sarah decided she wanted another hot chocolate. She stood up to head for the serving counter. 'You guys want another drink?'

Daisy and Aidan looked at each other, their telepathic link kicking in. Daisy grinned. 'Sure... anything that doesn't need a straw!'

———

I hope you enjoyed Daisy's second adventure. We will be eternally grateful if you can spare two minutes to leave a review on your preferred site. It really is very easy, and makes a huge difference; both as feedback to us, and to help potential readers know what others thought.

Thank you so much!

**Follow Daisy's adventures in the Third One, 'A Very Unexpected African Adventure',
(Catch a preview here...)**

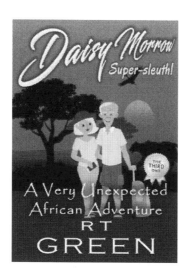

Here's a Sneaky Preview of the Third One...

'This is so exciting!'

'Everything is exciting to you,' grinned Daisy, sitting next to Sarah, in the aisle seat.

'Yes, but I've not led your exciting life,' she said, tearing her eyes away from the window and grinning back.

'Give it time, dear... you're getting there.'

Sarah, unable to not look out of the window for more than a second, watched as the airliner turned in a gentle bank to prepare for its final approach, and the lights of the runway at Entebbe airport filled her view.

'Oh.'

'Oh?'

'Um... what happens if we overshoot the landing? The runway seems to end right before the sea.'

'Lake dear, lake.'

'Well it looks like the sea... and it can drown you just as easily.'

Daisy patted her on the leg. 'Never mind dear, Aidan and me have had enough almost-drownings in recent weeks. We certainly wouldn't willingly put all our lives in danger.'

Aidan, sitting in the sear right behind, poked his head through and grinned. 'And why do you think we took out travel insurance?'

'You're not exactly helping, Aidan.'

Daisy saw the genuine look of concern on Sarah's face. 'Dear, it just doesn't happen, so take no notice of my dear husband doing his best to wind you up. And anyway, if we do overshoot the pilot just opens the throttles and we lift off again.'

'Still not helping, Daisy.'

'Sarah dear, just relax. There are plenty of buoyancy jackets.'

Sarah shook her head, and went back to watching the descent. The Emirates flight had taken fourteen hours in total with a short stop in Addis Ababa, so they were all more than ready to stretch their legs. For Sarah and Aidan, it was the first time they'd been to Africa, but Daisy had been before, three times in the distant past. But not to Uganda, so from that perspective it was an *exciting* new adventure for them all.

It had been a fraught seven days; the flights had been purchased straight away, but the Yellow Fever jabs and visas had taken several days to organise. Much to Daisy's impatience... if she'd had her way they would have been on a flight the day after she'd persuaded Burrows to grant Sarah time off.

The unexpected truth Adde Wambua let slip before his death was a much stronger lead than they'd ever had to help solve Celia's disappearance. In the space of three days before he died they'd discovered he was the one responsible for trafficking their daughter, and that she'd been sold to someone in Uganda.

He genuinely didn't know who, but he did know he was a high ranking government official. Which didn't help Daisy's cause. In Museveni's Uganda, such officials were almost always military, and protected by the army's rule of privacy. Everyone else got to know only what he wanted them to.

Extracting Celia from such a regime would not be easy, even if they could find out who it was who'd bought her.

They'd booked return flights for two weeks time, just because they would have to show the Ugandan officials they had a return flight booked. But none of them knew if two weeks would be enough time. The visas lasted forty-five days, and it might well be that return flights would have to be rebooked.

Both Aidan and Sarah knew Daisy would not go back to the UK until they'd found Celia. Even if she ended up having to stay there illegally.

The aircraft didn't overshoot the runway and end up at the bottom of Lake Victoria. As it taxied to the concourse outside the main building in the late-afternoon sunshine, Sarah gathered up her tablet, and looked at Daisy with wide eyes and flushed cheeks.

'I can't believe we're actually here!'

'Don't get too excited yet... we still have to endure a taxi-ride to Kampala.'

227

Aidan put a hand on her shoulder as they joined the disembarkation queue, and smiled reassuringly. 'Don't worry, Sarah. That main road is all asphalt, so as long as the driver avoids the potholes, we'll be alright.'

'And there was me thinking we'd be in the back of a cattle-truck.'

'Ok, point taken. I'll shut up now.'

Entebbe International Airport was actually quite smart. Way smaller than their departure point at Heathrow, it didn't really have any vast spaces with high ceilings. Much of it had been rebuilt just a few years ago, and their route through customs was quick and accompanied by big, friendly smiles. As they collected their luggage, Daisy slapped dry lips together.

'I'd love a coffee, dear. Look, the Crane Cafe is just over there. If it's ok to have ten minutes before we find a taxi, would you and Sarah grab drinks? I need the loo before taking in any more liquid.'

'Sounds like a plan. Come on Sarah... get a few Ugandan shillings out!'

Daisy headed to the toilets, but just as she was heading back to join the others, someone caught her eye. He looked Ugandan, middle-aged, and not very well. Dressed in a cream suit and patterned shirt, as she watched him he staggered slightly.

No one else noticed the man. The speakers had just announced boarding for the next flight to Nairobi, and most of the people in the waiting area were already hurrying to the gate. The man seemed like he was intending to join them, but he was a little way behind the crowd, and his legs looked like they were just about to collapse under him.

He grabbed the wall to hold himself up, but it wasn't enough. He fell to his knees. Daisy ran over to him. Still

228

there was no one else close. Fifteen feet from the exit doors, he must have entered through them just a minute or two ago, on his way to catch his flight. He had no luggage she could see, not even a hand-held case.

She knelt down beside him and reached out a hand, wrapped it around his shoulder. As he looked up to her with heavy eyes, she could feel his whole body shaking.

'Please...' he gasped in a soft Ugandan accent.

'Let me call someone,' said Daisy, realising he was in a bad way.

'No... no police...' he whispered, the corners of his mouth turning down as speaking became just as hard as moving.

'What can I do?' Daisy cried frantically.

He found a little movement, slipped a trembling hand into the pocket of his jacket. It looked like it was all he could do. And then he thrust a crumpled piece of paper into her hand, tried to say something.

The words wouldn't come. He let out a croaky kind of gasp, and one second later was flat out on the floor.

Daisy pressed a finger onto his neck, just as Aidan and Sarah came running up. 'Oh my god...' cried Sarah. 'Is he..?'

Daisy nodded. 'Yes, he's dead.'

Aidan looked around for some kind of divine inspiration. 'How long have we been here, dear?' Then he shook his head despondently. 'I'll find someone.'

A couple of airport police officers were already heading their way. Aidan met them, gave them the news. Before they reached the dead man, Daisy took a quick look at the note, and then shoved it hastily into her pocket.

'What's that?' whispered Sarah.

'Don't say anything yet, please? It was important enough for him to give it to me as his last act. It's just a name, but it clearly means something.'

229

'You should give it to the police, Daisy.'

'I know. But he begged me not to involve the police. We need to find out who he is, and why this was so crucial to him.'

'So you're telling me we've only been on African soil for an hour, and already there are two mysteries to solve, not one?'

'Yes dear, it rather looks that way.'

———

AND DO COME AND JOIN US!

We'd love you to become a VIP Reader.

Our intro library is the most generous in publishing!
Join our mail list and grab it all for free.
We really do appreciate every single one of you,
so there's always a freebie or two coming along,
news and updates, advance reads of new releases...

Head here to get started...
rtgreen.net

Printed in Great Britain
by Amazon